Tell Dad Not to Worry

by

ROBERT E. DONAHOE JR.

DORRANCE
PUBLISHING CO
EST. 1920
PITTSBURGH, PENNSYLVANIA 15238

Dorrance Publishing Co
585 Alpha Drive
Pittsburgh, PA 15238
Visit our website at *www.dorrancebookstore.com*

ISBN: 978-1-6393-7470-0
eISBN: 978-1-6393-7523-3

Tell Dad Not to Worry

A story of an individual's brief life from childhood to the ultimate sacrifice during World War II with the 2nd Marine Division (The Silent Second) in the Asiatic Pacific Theater

Guardian Angel Prayer

Guardian Angel from heaven so bright,
watching beside me to lead me aright,
Fold thy wings round me, and guard me with love,
softly sing songs to me of heaven above. Amen.

In Remembrance of
Jack "Jock" Donahoe
1/2/22 – 6/15/44
"Second to None"

Table of Contents

Author's Note

My Godfather, James Murphy, once said to me
"Stories live forever, as long as they are told."

It is for that reason I decided to tell this story in my own way, know-ing I would never get all the factual details correct because this per-son's life and those who knew him best have been gone for a long time now.

This story is about an uncle I never knew. I was not born until eleven years after his death. Yet I hold memories of him. Memories I formulated from stories my dad would tell me late at night around the kitchen table when I was in my early teens. I guess this is what my dad wanted from me, to be able to pass on the life and times of PFC Jack (Jock) Donahoe, USMC, 1942–1944.

So, several years later when I experienced my own brush with death and felt this pure absolute presence around me, it only steeled my resolve to put his story together the best I could. For I believe in some shape or form that my father's brother lives in me. He is living his life through me because he did not have that oppor-tunity to feel long enough, laugh long enough, love long enough, and just experience this world long enough to understand how fragile we really are.

Those that have encountered a near-death experience, will un-derstand the profound impact it can have on one's life. For those that have not, it is not something to take lightly. Sooner or later, it may happen to you and then you can decide. We take so much for granted.

This book is a work of partial fiction, but my uncle Jack and some of the characters and many of the events are real. Many of the stories have a factual basis to them. Some of the names and de-scriptions came from his Marine Corps scrapbook and letters to home. Other parts of Jack's life came from my dad telling me stories while sitting around the kitchen table late at night when I was in my early teens. The remainder was derived from actual historical events, research, and my imagination. I did my best to accurately describe the events that did or may have happened in his life. I only hope my best is good enough.

One last thing. When my uncle Jack wrote letters to his brother and sister, he always ended it with: "Tell Dad not to worry."

Dedication

This book is dedicated in memory of my dad, Robert E. Donahoe, Sr.

While his brother, my uncle Jack, enlisted in the Marine Corps, my dad joined the Army, served in the Rhineland, Central Europe, the Ardennes and participated in the Battle of the Bulge in December of 1944. He is a Purple Heart recipient. He was a remarkable man.

Since two wars were raging at the same time in different parts of the world, news did not travel as fast as it does these days. My dad did not receive word of his brother being killed in action until three months after it happened as he was fighting in Europe.

I also want to pay tribute to some other remarkable men I have known and admired through the early years of my life. To my two childhood best friends' fathers, John Kelly, and George Brady, Sr. These men saw action during World War II. They experienced the horrors of combat, fear of their own demise, but most importantly the realization that a bond of trust must exist amongst their brethren if they have any chance of surviving. They kept their own personal stories untold for their own reasons. These men made it home and put their tribulations behind them to raise families. They are all deceased now.

The other remarkable man is my high school wrestling coach, Roger Shores. He inspired us to give 100 percent in everything we do whether on the mat or in life. "When the going gets tough, the tough get going," he would always say.

If you believe in fate, the timing was a godsend. Just two weeks prior of being recruited to join the wrestling team, or should I say, "coerced to fill an empty weight class," my little world turned upside down. I was walking home from school with a couple of friends when a Chevy Suburban pulls over with my dad in the passenger side wearing a mask. Its only 2:30 in the afternoon and he would normally be at work, but when I saw the mask, I knew something was wrong. He asked me to come home as he had some news to share. That news was not good. He contracted tuberculosis and was being admitted to the Norfolk County Respiratory Hospital in

Braintree Highlands. He would remain there isolated in a quarantine ward throughout my sophomore year. They treated him with experimental drugs in the hope of slowing the spread of this disease. Ultimately, after almost a year of being treated with these new wonder drugs, the bacterial infection was still spreading. The only solution was to remove the diseased portion of his lung. (Our dad's mother, Nora, died from tuberculosis when he was an infant.)

It was a trying time for me as my older siblings were away in college, my younger siblings were in elementary school, and my mom did not work or drive. We had to rely on our neighbors for almost everything. Perhaps the toughest thing for me was not being able to visit our dad in the hospital because of the highly communicable nature of TB. No one under the age of eighteen was allowed in. So, my two youngest siblings and I could only see our dad from his third-story window in the rear of the hospital on weekends. That is if my older sister or brother were able to get home from college during a weekend or we were fortunate enough to have a neighbor drive us.

I remember we would have to yell to each other to be heard. The year was 1970 and at that time tuberculosis was still the number one deadliest infectious disease in the world. So, at the age of fifteen my coach filled that void. His guidance and encouragement gave me purpose and forged many of the ideals and ethics I carry to this day.

One thing I learned while growing up: "Courage is measured not how you stand, but how you get up after you have fallen."

I realize many people have had their own tragedies in their lifetime and so many have suffered and endured much worse than my family, but holding it in for such a long time can wear on you. There comes a time when you just got to let it out.

Acknowledgments

Special thanks to the Murphy Family. Jim was my Godfather and saw my uncle Jack and dad go off to war. Jim was instrumental in reminding me of what we are all capable of doing. His own published writings gave me the confidence to try something I would have never dreamt of doing.

Unfortunately, Jim passed away before this got published but the continued support from his family got me across the finish line.

Lastly, but most importantly, I am grateful for having my loving wife, "Shirley," who has stayed by me during my most trying times. When I need to lean on her, she is always there to hold me up.

Introduction

Allston-Brighton was once known as Little Cambridge up until 1807 when it was formally established as a suburb of Boston by the Massachusetts Legislature. Its main commerce back then was the cattle markets and horticulture. By the mid-nineteenth century this village just west of Boston was predominantly a Yankee and Irish community with a minority of Italians and Jews. Then by the 1870s, a transformation was underway as the town fathers wanted to invest in public facilities including streetcar accessibility. The best way to promote this progressive movement and by making this area a commuter suburb was to relocate and consolidate the dozens of small-scale slaughterhouses and its by-products of tallow, oil, and fertilizers into a large stockyard adjacent to the Boston & Albany rail line in North Brighton. By the mid-1870s, the town was formally annexed and became a neighborhood to the City of Boston. The beginning of the twentieth century saw a "second wave" of newer Irish immigrants making the area their home and by the 1920s many other ethnicities such as Asians, Hispanics, and Afro-Americans migrated to the area. Brighton was in the crossroads of becoming a gateway for high-quality suburban development.

During this time, Brighton took on greater significance. A more diverse, ethnic populace took root and flourished throughout World War II.

This cultural diversity was evident everywhere in the community, especially in the commercial sections of town. These "new immigrants" considered themselves blessed to be in a land where freedom prevailed, and prosperity could be achieved with hard work. This would be the generation that would instill the "can-do" attitude for generations to come. The emergence of these new immigrants from Brighton and the surrounding areas of Watertown and Newton, as well as the other "immigrant quarters" of greater Boston would have a significant impact to the outcome of World War II.

Serving in the Armed Forces of the United States demonstrated their resolve and commitment for a country they dearly loved and to a way of life others could only dream about all around the world.

Jack W. Donahoe's grandparents were Irish immigrants on both sides of the family tree. They arrived in America around the turn of the century and settled in the greater Boston area where the bustling textile industry, shoe manufacturing, garment industry, food and produce, and related trades offered the greatest opportunity for fair and steady work. By the time the 1920s came along, the Donahoes and the Horans were well established in the community.

It was right here in Brighton where William Donahoe, a young energetic law student met Nora Horan; they married in 1919 and had their three children. Just sixteen months after their third child was born, Nora passed away, a victim of tuberculosis.

Jack, the second of three siblings was born January 2, 1922, at Saint Elizabeth's Hospital in Brighton. They made their home on North Beacon Street near the Allston town line.

Jack's father was a devout Catholic attending Saint Columbkille's church every Sunday and helping at the parish when he was not out of town with work. But Father led two lives. An immensely proud and somewhat arrogant man, William Donahoe had a sharp mind and a sharper edge that would ultimately lead him to a controversial lifestyle. Later in his life these traits led him down a path of self-indulgence, but fortunately all three children were instilled with the noble and just values Father was brought up with. Their religious upbringing also set the tone on which Jack would lead his life. So, when Father was called upon to apply his trade as a lawyer working for the government in Washington, DC, Jack's two aunts along with his uncle would take care of him, his brother, and older sister.

Aunt Lil and Uncle Tom never had children of their own, and Aunt Peg never married. They welcomed the duties of being surrogate parents. The children were also fortunate to have many other relatives close by like Uncle Frank and Aunt Rose from the Murphy/Horan clan as well as William and Lena from the Garvin/Horan side of the family. This rich family heritage provided a solid foundation of love and compassion for the young Donahoes.

Sunday was church day for the family. They would all go to the 9:00 a.m. Mass at Saint Columbkille's down on Market Street, then to the cemetery in Brookline to pay their respects to their mother. Jack was five years old when she died. His memory of her was vague, but what he did remember was a frail woman always covered with a blanket. She had this terrible cough, and her hankie often was covered with blood. She needed someone to help her get out of her favorite rocking chair or her bed. Her illness never seemed to overwhelm the children. They were accustomed to it. It was their way of life, doing whatever needed to be done to help ease their mother's suffering.

Jack could sense something was amiss, but still too young to grasp the gravity of their mother's condition. Brother Bobby was just an infant. Once Nora passed, Jack would ask his sister Evelyn if Mother were still sleeping and when would she be waking up. It seemed to be especially hard on Jack, for he had the most difficult time understanding why all the other children attended church with their mothers. Jack never cried or showed his feelings. He did not want to appear frightened in front of his family. Their father was too proud to have a Donahoe son show emotion, especially crying. To him it was a sign of weakness.

After their mother passed away, the three children attended the parochial school system at Saint Columbkille's from first grade to eighth. Evelyn was two years older than Jack and Jack three years older than Bobby. Although each were supposed to be two grades apart in school, Jack had difficulties with his motor vocabulary skills and was held back to repeat the second grade. It did not seem to bother Jack. He was small for his age. In fact, his little brother Bobby was the same size as Jack when Bobby started school. One thing was clear, though, by the time Jack turned twelve years of age, it was obvious to everybody that he possessed natural athletic ability and skill. Every sport he participated in came easy except for swimming. He was a sinker, so he learned to hold his breath for an exceptionally long time.

When it came time for pick-up baseball games down behind Smith's Field near Faneuil Street, he always got chosen first or second. But his true love was hockey. Once the ice was thick enough down on Chandler's Pond, Jack was the first one out there. It was almost a mile away from home, but he made the trek by foot every chance he could. The family always called him Jackie, but the older boys gave him the nickname of Jock or Jocko. No one is sure why this nickname was given, but it is believed to be enthroned upon him as a symbol of his toughness. Nobody could catch the speed-ster. His agility and determination were noticed by all the other kids. He also kept to himself, never looking for attention or seeking praise. He was introverted but warmed up to others rather quickly especially if it had to do with sports.

Jack kept a close eye on his little brother Bob while Ev made sure they both stayed in line during their years at Saint Columbkille's Catholic Elementary School. Even the nuns took note of their pro-tection for each other. Walking to school was their primary mode of transportation and luckily their home was less than a half mile away.

As anyone can surmise attending a Catholic school during the 1930s, discipline from the nuns was dispensed without any fear of retribution or condemnation from the parents or for that matter any organization. It was a different time back then.

In 1937, Jack entered Brighton High School. He was now fifteen years old, weighed about one hundred and ten pounds and stood five feet, four inches tall. Yet even at this unimpressive stature, Jack earned a reputation of being one tough SOB. Because of his rather slight size and build, there was always some bigger or older kid that would try to bully Jock. Their attempts were in vain. It seemed like every time some punk tried to give Jock a hard time, they ended up on the short end of the stick. This ended with Jock spending much of his time in detention after school for all four years he attended. But it did not bother Jock too much. At least he had no reason not to do his homework.

This never happened at St. Columbkille's. The sisters ruled with an iron hand and a heavy yardstick. But at the public schools, espe-cially at the high school level, discipline was a little less strict. There always seemed to be someone that thought they were tougher than Jock, or that he was just lucky. So, Jock had to defend himself on more than one occasion.

Story has it he never lost a fight. No matter the size of his oppo-nent or the odds stacked against him, he always would come out on top. Not once did he ever brag about his athletic ability. He hated to be the center of attention and just shrugged off any accolades di-rected his way.

Nobody ever taught or trained him to fight; he was just that type of individual with a keen sense of awareness and reflexes like a cat.

On one lazy, hot Saturday afternoon walking with his buddies towards the stockyard as they routinely did to check out the hundreds of cattle in the corals, a couple of older kids were passing by when one of them suckered punched Jock from behind. Jock went down but did not stay there for long. Within seconds he had the perpetrator down on his knees screaming for forgiveness while his accomplice hightailed it back over the North Beacon Street Bridge to safer ground.

His father told him once that the big guys may have big balls, but the little guy has all balls. That expression made an impression he aimed to live by for the rest of his brief life.

Chapter I

Age of Innocence

Hockey tryouts would start the day they would come back from Thanksgiving break and Jock wanted to be in the best shape possible. So, he ran. He ran at least five miles every day except on Saturdays and Sundays. He worked every Saturday at Hurley's Dry Cleaners on Market Street. It was always hot and the work boring, but it would give Jock enough money to buy the Hyde Super Flyer ice skates he has been wanting since last year. Besides, there was this cute girl that worked there on Saturdays also. Jock always wanted to ask her out on a date but could not muster enough nerve to do so. The one crack in his armor.

On the first day of tryouts, there must have been sixty boys ready to impress the coaches with their skills and abilities by any means possible. Jock felt nervous only briefly while waiting for his turn. Not knowing when he would get his turn on the ice was the hardest part. You could just tell the coaches were getting quite frazzled with trying to sort out the best of the best since just about every kid in town skated or played hockey in the winter.

Finally, they called out the last group of kids onto the ice. Jock was given a blue shirt to put on over his gear. They were the blue team. Luckily, two of his buddies were on the same team. They played together since they were little and knew each other's style of play. Jock was hoping this would give them a little advantage over the other boys. Jock got to play right wing, his buddy Phil was playing center, and his other buddy Eddy was on defense.

The puck dropped to the ice and the red team quickly seized control and regrouped behind the net. Their passing was flawless as they prepared to set up for the drive to the net.

Jock knew that his team would be in trouble if they couldn't switch the momentum back to their side as quickly as possible, so he would have to anticipate their every move.

The red team's center attempted a quick wrist-flick pass to his left-winger that was barreling in on Jock. With a calculated risk,

Jock maneuvered between the red team's center and left winger and with an outstretched reach was able to intercept the puck.

"I'm clear!" yelled Phil, and with one continuous motion, Jock got the pass off to his center. Gathering the puck in close to his body and knowing any second would get checked by a red team opponent, Phil looked up only to find the red team's center had just taken a spill courtesy of Big Eddy. Phil made for the open lane and crossed the blue line, leaving the puck trailing behind for his left-wing teammate. The left-winger scooped it up and followed Phil down the middle. Phil split to his left and blocked the defenseman, giving Eddy sufficient time to let go of a crackling slapshot.

The goalie was ready and deflected the blistering shot, but as if orchestrated, Jock slid in behind their defense to pick off the deflection and shoot a high wrist shot over the goalie's left shoulder for a score.

In that split second as Jock released the shot, he got hammered by a 180-pound gorilla nicknamed Moose. He was a sophomore that didn't make the team last year, so he had to make a big impression this time around.

Jock was stunned but got right back up so that the coaches could see it did not affect him, although he was a little wobbly as he searched for his stick.

Phil skated up to him and said, "Holy cripes, Jock, are you okay? You took a helluva hit."

Jock picked up his hockey stick and spit a little blood onto the ice. "Never better; let's go do that again."

For the next couple of minutes, both teams were unable to score or do anything that resembled dominance on the ice. The whistle blew and off they came. Once in the dressing room, one of the coaches came over to see if Jock was all right, and to praise him for his heads-up play. "All you got to do is put on a few pounds and you will impress a lot of people."

"Thanks, Coach; I'm working on gaining some weight."

The next morning, Jock, Phil, and Big Eddy scrambled down to the boy's locker room to see if the sheet for the next round of players was posted. After reading down the list of names, they let out a sigh of relief. Their names were all on the list. At least they made it to the next and final round.

The final tryouts were exhaustive. Jock could not remember when he was that tired. Every muscle in his body ached, probably from that viscous hip check he received the other day from Moose.

It seemed like Jock was on the ice for the last twenty minutes. The game was tied at 3 to 3. Jock hadn't gotten any of the goals but assisted on two of them. Time was running out. He knew that he had to start taking chances if there was any chance of making the team.

As the puck dropped from the coach's hand in the face-off circle, Phil wrested control of the puck and slid it back to Eddy on defense. Eddy coveted the puck and retreated around the net to try to get some momentum going but got clobbered by Moose. It seemed like this kid had little skating ability but sure knew how to intimidate people.

Collecting the puck, Moose swung around the opposite side of the net and tried to take a point-blank slap shot right at the goal. Realizing that the game could be over in a moment's notice, Jock gave it all he had and checked Moose into the boards. It wasn't the prettiest check but effective enough for Moose to lose the puck and Eddy reclaimed it.

With only a half a minute on the clock, Eddy skates down the right side and leads a passing shot to Phil. With the left winger trailing just a little behind, Phil drifts to the right a bit, makes a complete 180-degree turn and passes it over to his left-wing man.

The pass was perfect, sliding between the red team's defenseman's legs and right on to the tip of the left-winger's stick where he winds up and takes the hardest slapshot he could muster catching the upper left corner for the goal. They raise their sticks and cajole each other for the fine teamwork displayed. The assistant coach skates over to them and gives them a job well done. If that play didn't lock up a place on the team for these three, nothing would.

The following day they were not disappointed. All three made the cut. They were now part of Brighton Highs "Warriors" hockey team. Phil pulls Jock and Eddy aside from the crowd of hopeful hockey players. "This calls for a toast gentleman."

That evening, on their way home from tryouts, Phil, Eddy and Jock stopped in at Pews to celebrate their achievement. It was sort of a ritual for these three since they were in the first grade. They would go after a baseball game on a Saturday morning, coming back from bowling on a Friday night, or even after watching a movie at the Egyptian. These three were inseparable. They also got into the typical trouble most teenagers had an ability for.

One time, Phil was able to acquire a pint of 80 proof vodka and a half pint of brandy. The three of them would climb the emergency fire escape to the top of the Stockyard and sit behind the parapet out of view, drinking and throwing whatever was available at the livestock cars along the rail spur behind the slaughterhouse. Often, they would get the cattle so riled up that the animals would kick holes in the side of the building and fence. This ultimately led to the police investigating the nuisance, but they would never catch the three of them as they hid up on the roof behind the parapet. The police never had a clue as to whom or what caused the commotion.

On another occasion, they were not so lucky. It seemed every Friday night the boys would walk out of the bowling alley with either some bowling shoes or a bowling ball. The problem was what do with all this stuff and where to hide it?

Well, they were soon liberated from this problem when Officer O'Reilly followed them all the way back to Phil's home where he had this old, dilapidated storage shed in his backyard. As the boys were unloading their prized possessions, Officer O'Reilly and two squad cars flashed their powerful searchlights and turned on their sirens at 11:00 p.m. in this quiet little neighborhood on Elmira Street.

All three were released on personal recognizance but had to return everything and work at the bowling alley for the entire summer with no pay. They had to sweep, buff, and polish every square inch of flooring, repair any damaged candlepins, clean the back alley, and the restrooms. Not to mention deodorizing all those smelly shoes every evening after closing. The following summer, the boys never went near a bowling alley.

During Jock's four years at Brighton High, he was a stand-out in hockey. Making the All-Star team three years in a row and winning the league championship his senior year. Although a few grades apart, Jack's younger brother Bobby also made the team his freshman year and on occasion played together in the same line up. Jack was very proud of that. Jock's junior and senior year won him laurels with the school administration although his grades were marginal at best. Jock even won the MVP award for their division in his senior year. He had never expected that. It is believed that Jock still holds the title for most assists in the Brighton High record books.

When the college recruiters came searching for talent, Jock was overlooked because of his size. He was 5 feet 6 inches tall and weighed all of 125 pounds his senior year. They felt he would get hurt against the bigger and stronger guys and therefore not able to contribute to the overall scheme of things at the college level.

Nonetheless, with his wiry frame, massive hands, and intense steel blue eyes, not to mention the reputation he acquired over the last four years, he had earned the respect of his peers. Jock's size and weight along with his quiet, introverted personality lent to the belief that some of the bigger guys could intimidate him. So, when some punk challenged that respect, well it didn't take long for that perception to change.

Probably the most prevalent trait about Jock was his demeanor. It was hard to get a word out of him unless you were a close pal. His loyalty to his friends ran deep. Always there standing side by side if and when needed.

Jock also had difficulty asking girls out for a date. He was handsome but a little introverted to some extent and just couldn't get up enough nerve to ask girls out. He was always fearful the girl would say no and go tell her other girlfriends. So, he waited until he was really sure about someone. That someone would eventually be his confidant, his best friend, his girl.

Chapter II

Lessons of Life

It was September 1940 and America was just getting back on its feet after the depression years. The industrial sector was ramping up especially with the threat of global conflicts. America sensed it was on the verge of fighting two wars in two different parts of the globe. Jock was entering his senior year at Brighton High School.

He knew his chances of getting a scholarship to play hockey were slim and his grades were one notch above failing. In his heart he knew he wanted to be a soldier. He loved watching the recruiting advertisements shown in between the feature films at the Egyptian Theatre located on Washington Street down in Brighton Center. It seemed so exciting and adventurous. He figured that if war broke out, he would enlist and go back to school later. He was certain if he stayed in high school, any war could be over by the time graduation came around and he did not want to miss any of the action. There would be plenty of time to finish his education after the war. But his father would have nothing to do with it. Jock's dad was a naval officer in World War I and did not want his sons to experience the cruelties of war. But war would not come to America at this time. So, Jock persevered and stayed in school graduating in May of 1941. He continued working through the Summer and Fall at the dry cleaners during the week and helping his uncle at the family quarry just over the state line in Brookline, New Hampshire on weekends. It was about an hour and a half ride each way which made for awfully long days. It gave Jock time to clear his head and think of what lies ahead for him.

Handling those large pieces of granite was dangerous work but it gave him the thick forearms unusual for a person of his size and frame. It definitely helped him with wrist shots during his hockey years.

When the Imperial Japanese Navy attacked Pearl Harbor on that fateful Sunday morning of December 7, 1941, Jock and his family heard about it that late Sunday afternoon on their radio in the parlor. Father turned pale as a ghost when he heard the broadcast. He turned to Jock and said, "I saw this coming. It was only a matter of time. We should have been better prepared." He knew Jock wanted to enlist but his dad was able to dissuade him up until now. "If you want to enlist, you have my blessing if that is what you really want." Jock did not smile or say anything. He just sat there respecting his father's solitude. He knew that this was not the time or place to celebrate. It was a time for praying for all of those who lost their lives that day.

The following day, with no prospect of a college scholarship Jock and his pal Eddy headed straight for the Marine Recruitment Center across the Charles River in Allston. The line extended for what seemed like a mile.

When they entered the building and filled out the paperwork, Eddy went into one line and Jock into another.

Eddy's physical examination went without a hitch, but Jock's was a different story. The physician examining Jock asked him if he had been in an accident or had been in a fight.

"Just a couple of fights here and there. Why?" responded Jock.

"You've got a punctured eardrum. I'm sorry, son. I must give you a 4-F. That means you are unfit for duty. I'm really sorry." Jock was devastated. He must have received the punctured eardrum in one of his many fights over the years.

Eddy was just finishing filling out the forms when Jock came over to tell him the bad news. Eddy could not believe it. "This is what you wanted to do more than me! I'm sorry, Jock." Eddy picked up his forms and proceeded to the recruiter's desk. "Jock, I hope you don't mind, but I'm still gonna go through with it."

"I understand. Don't let me hold you back. I know how much this means to you too. I'll be fine. I'll just find another way to join."

Eddy and Jock parted, one getting into the next line for processing the other one headed for the door to begin that long walk home feeling cheated. All he ever really wanted was to make a difference. Now his dreams were shattered. No college scholarship for hockey. No enlistment into the Marine Corp. It demoralized him to a point that he did not want to talk or see anyone. Life just did not seem fair. Cripes, Moose got a scholarship to play at Holy Cross the year before and he was the dumbest kid in the school! Not only that, but

Jock could skate circles around him!

Some of Jock's other buddies like Phil and Mike were planning to enlist in the fall. This way they could have a little fun during the summer before going off to war. Now his best friend Eddy was on his way to be a Marine. He felt more like an outcast. So, at nineteen years of age Jock decided it was time for a change. He knew the most difficult thing to do lay ahead of him. How would he tell his girl Jeanne that he was leaving? He had immense feelings for her and wanted their relationship to continue but could not bear the embarrassment of being rejected by the military.

That evening Jock said goodbye to his sweetheart of two years. She was heartbroken. That same evening Jock told his family. Father was sympathetic but did not ask him to reconsider. He knew his son had to do things his way. That was the one thing about Jock. He had the trait of a typical stubborn Irishman. For the next few days, he got his responsibilities in order. He gave his notice at the dry cleaners, closed out his savings account at the bank, which comprised of $350 dollars and said his good-byes to relatives and friends.

On Saturday with a light snow falling, Jock boarded the train to Groton, Connecticut with everything he could fit in a large duffel bag and an old suitcase that had to be tied with rope to keep from springing open. He had read in the newspaper that Pratt & Whitney had many job openings at their engine factory in Groton, Connecticut. Pratt & Whitney had lost many employees to the draft and were in dire need of machinists and drafters and Jock was rather good with a pencil and paper. He thought once of studying architecture in college. However, his first objective was to become a Marine, just like those in the recruiting advertisements and just like his ex-girlfriend's father. That would have to wait for now.

Hired immediately at the engine manufacturer's facility, Jock's position was that of Apprentice Draftsman and earned him $0.55 an hour. He was also able to move into an apartment with a couple of other guys just two blocks from the facility. Things were looking better. The rent was $18 dollars a month for his share of the apartment, and he did not need a car. He and his roommates would walk to and from work and take the local trolley car to other parts of the city on weekends. Jock was able to put a few dollars away. Maybe after the war he would go back to school and become an architect after all.

For the first six months of 1942, work at the Pratt & Whitney facility went by without much fanfare. Jock got along with the rest of the guys, most of them much older than himself. He wrote home once a week and twice a week to his ex-girlfriend. She replied to all his letters.

Come the Summer of 1942, there was some gossip at the factory regarding the armed forces re-evaluating their qualifications for enlistments. No official word but Jock kept his ears open.

He also read the newspapers daily and kept a radio beside his drafting table in work. Company rules prohibited the use of radios during the work shift, but his boss allowed him to listen to it during lunchtime. He listened intently on the progress of the war. It fascinated him to hear about the battle at Midway and the Aleutian Islands campaign. He heard about the exploits of Howling Mad Dog Smith and Chesty Puller.

Listening to those valiant and brave stories that came from the bloody fighting by the First and Second Marine Divisions, he knew right there and then that was what he wanted to be a part of. "Someday, someday I'm going to be a part of something big."

In the early Fall of 1942, Jock kept on hearing persistent rumors about the armed forces granting exemptions to young men that may not have qualified for active service due to minor medical abnormalities. Jock was now twenty years of age and felt this may be his last chance to become a Marine. So, one Saturday, he went down to the local recruiting / medical evaluation center in Groton and tried again. This time he got cleared. The day was October 11th, 1942. Since he was born in Massachusetts, Jack was instructed to go back home and officially report for enlistment in Springfield, Massachusetts on November 5th.

Jock gave his notice the following Monday at the Pratt and Whitney plant and packed up his belongings and left for home that Friday afternoon. When he arrived home that evening, the only two that were in the house were his younger brother Bobby and his sister Evelyn. As soon as Jock started to tell both, Evelyn burst into tears. She didn't want her brother to go off to war. She just had a dream the night before about Jock, and it wasn't good. She dreamt

Jock drowned when an enemy torpedo struck the ship he was on, and it sunk to the bottom of the sea with no survivors.

Of course, Jock had to console Evelyn telling her that he could outswim everybody in the neighborhood and that he would wear a life preserver on the entire voyage to wherever he was going. Everyone knew swimming was not one of Jock's strong suits.

Brother Bobby was excited but a little concerned too. He knew his big brother could take care of himself no matter what came his way. But Bobby also knew that trouble followed Jock. It seemed like he was always the one to get caught when the guys he hung around with decided to perform a prank or get into some mischief down on Oak Square on a Friday night.

Nonetheless, Jock had no second thoughts on what he was doing and could not wait till father got home from his trip down in Washington, DC. He would get little sleep that night as his mind raced with the visions of what lay ahead in basic training and then off to war.

On Saturday morning Jock was awakened as father shook him gently. "When did you get home?" Jock sat upright in his bed trying to get oriented after a sleepless night. "I have been home for a couple of hours, why? "I noticed some of your bag's downstairs in the parlor."

"What are you doing home? Were you fired or something?"

"No, Dad, I quit. You see I went to the recruiting office in Groton where they had a medical staff to evaluate if I can be cleared and this time, they accepted me! So, I am enlisting. I'm scheduled to report at 22 Tremont Row in Scollay Square on November 3rd. There will be a bus there to take us out to Springfield for formal enlistment and filling out family medical history forms. The next day we will be taking a train to Trenton, New Jersey and on to Philadelphia. We then change trains bound for somewhere in South Carolina. Then our final leg will be a bus ride to Parris Island for basic training, isn't that great?"

There was a moment of silence before his dad could say anything, and then he blurted out "That is great, I'm proud of you but how did you get by the qualification review?"

Jock was now fully awake and able to explain with a clear mind. "They are exempting the hearing standards so that all you have to do is pass the test in one ear and you're in," responded Jock. "Jesus, Mary and Joseph! What will come next? I suppose they will take sixteen-year-olds like your brother Bobby!"

"Don't worry, Bobby will finish high school first and by then the war will be over."

"I hope to God you are right, Jock; I hope to God you are right."

Fifteen minutes later the family gathered around the parlor table. Bobby was getting ready to high tail it over to Carl's Supermarket on Arlington Street to deliver groceries. Evelyn was preparing sandwiches for Bobby and herself. It was getting to be a ritual for them. She would come home every Friday night from Regis College in Weston, Massachusetts. Evelyn had taken an internship at a small accounting firm in Allston on the weekends and was hoping upon graduating from Regis College there would be a permanent job there for her. Regis was only 10 miles away, so it made it convenient.

She was starting her third year there and was able to scrape up enough money to get her own car. The biggest concern was that she was a terrible driver. Jock and Bobby refused to drive with her anyplace. She would hit the brakes if she saw anything remotely resembling a living creature within a four-mile radius and pop the clutch so hard to get going again they would be holding their necks when exiting the car. Jock and Bobby were careful not to upset Evelyn though. Whenever Evelyn offered either of them a ride someplace, they would always say they were going in the other direction.

Father had some business over at Gillette in South Boston that morning. Gillette had suffered during the late '30s and early '40's due to the government embargoing any steel shipped to Axis powers or the Empire of the Rising Sun because of the looming threat of the war. Therefore, their steel supplies were regulated by the government which impacted their bottom line. In order to survive in business during these times, Gillette converted some of their razor blade manufacturing to producing shell casings for the war effort. Father's role was to review and ensure all the legal details were appropriately worked out.

Jock was making plans to visit his old girlfriend from high school, Jeanne Daye. He hadn't seen her in over five months and figured she would not take the news very well. He was reminiscing about the first time he met her, their first date and especially the first time he met her dad.

Jeanne Daye lived on Union Street down on the south side of town, so Jock decided to take the Market Street Trolley to Union Square and walk the rest of the way. It was only a few blocks from where he used to work at the dry cleaners. In fact, that is where he met Jeanne. She did not go to Brighton High like most of the kids in the area. She attended Boston Latin, a prestigious school but also one with a rather snobbish reputation at the time. It was a school that could almost guarantee getting into a fine college such as Boston College or Holy Cross.

Her father, a retired Master Sargent in the Marine Corp for 20 years was now teaching algebra at Boston Latin. He was only 5 foot 9 inches but had those cold steel gray piercing eyes that could cut through you in a moment's notice. He was also the US Marine Corp middleweight champion in boxing for 6 years. Mr. Daye could not be intimidated by anybody. The good news was that he liked Jock. Jock remembered the first time he met Mr. Daye. It was an extremely hot afternoon in the middle of July. Both Jeanne and Jock were working in the back room of the dry cleaners when he walked in with three pairs of brown pants and three long sleeved white shirts. Jock remembered thinking; "Who would wear long sleeved shirts on days like this?" and there Mr. Daye stood, in a long sleeve white shirt and solid brown tie looking cool and in control as anyone Jock had ever seen.

The owner of the shop greeted Mr. Daye at the front desk. "Good afternoon, Mr. Daye. It's a hot one today is it not?"

"Yes... yes, it is, Mr. Hurley, a hot day it is. Would you mind if I spoke to my daughter for a moment?"

"No, not at all, I'll go get her." The shop was not large, so both Jeanne and Jock overheard some of the conversation at the front counter, so Jeanne grab Jock's hand and pulled him out to meet her father. Jock was a little embarrassed because Jeanne would not let go of his hand.

"Hi, Daddy, I want you to meet someone. This is Jock Donahoe. He lives over on North Beacon Street. Jock asked if he could take me out to the matinee tomorrow afternoon." At that moment Jock was petrified! He hadn't even asked Jeanne for a date yet, but she guessed right.

Mr. Daye extended his hand towards Jock, so Jock immediately extended his. Mr. Daye's grip was like a vise. Jock could feel his hand sweating as Mr. Daye's hand enveloped his.

"Nice to meet you. Are you one of William Donahoe's boys? Your father helped me with a small matter several years ago. I haven't seen him since."

"Yes, err... yes, sir," stuttered Jock. "He travels to Washington, DC a lot now. He is working for the government."

"Is that so? Well, give him my regards when you see him."

"I will, sir."

"Well, Daddy... can I go to the Egyptian with Jock tomorrow?" The Egyptian was the theater located in Brighton Center.

"Sure, sure you can, just be home at a decent hour. Oh yeah, I almost forgot why I wanted to talk to you. I'm going away for a few weeks starting this Monday. So, your mother is going to need your help around the house and with your little sister while I'm gone. Don't make any plans, okay?"

"Yes, Daddy. Where are you going?"

Mr. Daye looked at Jock first, then into Jeanne's eyes. "It seems like the US Government can't function without me. They want me to go down to Parris Island to help restructure training procedures for the incoming recruits. It appears they need to push them through faster so they can be ready for any military action that might come. Don't worry, honey. I'm only gonna be gone for two weeks."

"As long as you are not going off to war," responded Jeanne. That was a moment Jock would never forget.

On his way over to Jeanne's house, Jock decided to stop at the dry cleaners to see Mr. Hurley one last time before he went off. Mr. Hurley was standing behind the counter, talking to one of his regular patrons. That was the great thing about Mr. Hurley, he always had a warm disposition even when business was bad. He always made you feel welcomed and comfortable, almost like your favorite uncle.

The last customer had just left the shop when Mr. Hurley looked up and smiled. "Jock, how are you? It has been a long time. Come over here; let's take a look at you." The two shook hands and then Mr. Hurley reached closer and gave Jock a hug. "You know Jock;

business has not been the same since you left. I never get the pretty girls coming in anymore to drop off their school uniforms and to see if you were working. Now I just get their mothers and fathers coming in." Mr. Hurley's sons were both in the navy. One was serving on the battleship USS Maryland, and the other on the destroyer, USS Ringgold, both in the pacific theater. Jock had known them before they went off to enlist. They worked at the dry-cleaning shop when Pearl Harbor was attacked. The next morning, they were the first two in line at the naval recruiting office across the Charles River in Watertown.

"So, Mr. Hurley, I'd like you to be the first to know, outside of my family of course, that I've joined the Marines. They changed the qualification criteria so now all I had to do was pass the hearing test in one ear."

"My-my," said Mr. Hurley. "What will all those girls do when they find out? You are definitely going to make a lot of them cry."

"Don't worry about that, Mr. Hurley. I am sure they will wait for me when I return." They both chuckled.

"Well, I know one certain girl who is going to miss you," whispered Mr. Hurley.

"I know. I am on my way over to see her now. I just wanted to stop in to say goodbye."

"Wait one-minute, Jock, I have something for you."

Mr. Hurley went into the back room for a moment. He heard Mr. Hurley talking to himself, and boxes being moved and then a pause. When he came back out, he was carrying a small wooden box. He opened it and pulled out a somewhat tarnished metal cross on a neck chain.

"Here, I want you to have this. You see when my two boys went off to fight the Japanese; I bought each of them a cross. I decided to get one for myself so there would always be this connection while they were gone. I thought this way I could be near them all the time, but now I see this could serve a better purpose. Please, take it. You will be doing my sons and me a great honor."

Jock reluctantly extended his hand and placed it around his neck. "Thank you, Mr. Hurley, I will wear it with pride. And don't worry, I will take good care of it and return it to you when I come home."

"Jock, you have been like a son to me. Wear it always. It will protect you like it has for my sons. They have seen much action. Many of their fellow sailors have died, but they have been safe and healthy."

"I will," said Jock. "God is on our side. Thank you so much." With that Jock gave Mr. Hurley a huge embrace and went off to find the girl he left behind before embarking on his new journey.

Upon reaching the walkway to 164 Union Street, Jock noticed someone at the window looking out. It was Jeanne's little sister, Maggie. As soon as Maggie saw Jock, she let out a holler that Jock and probably others could hear from blocks away. Jock was a little embarrassed at the commotion, but what the heck; it is nice to be popular.

Maggie greeted Jock first at the front steps with a huge hug. Jock picked her up and swung her around like a ride on a Ferris wheel. Jock couldn't help but marvel at the surroundings. Their home was huge, three stories tall with a porch that wrapped around the entire front and right side. The third floor was turned into an apartment since there was only the four of them in the Daye family and they did not need all the space.

There was a swinging bench on the front porch that Jock and Jeanne used to sit on for hours and hours on end just looking up at the stars and talking about what they would like to do with their lives. Jeanne always wanted to be a nurse and hoped to work in a pediatric ward of a hospital, preferably Saint Elizabeth's as it was just a half-mile from their home. She loved children and knew since she was a little girl that she would become a nurse someday... just like her mother.

Jock kept Maggie in his arms. "Look at you," said Jock. "You have gotten so beautiful! I bet all the boys are asking you on dates."

"No, silly, I'm only nine," responded Maggie. "Besides, I'm going to marry Andrew when I grow up." Andrew lived next door. They have been childhood sweethearts since kindergarten although Andrew did not have a clue.

"Oh, that's right; I forgot," Jock said with a grin.

Just then, Jeanne walked out through the front door. "Hey, Maggie, I'm getting jealous. You already have a boyfriend; this one is mine." Jock put Maggie down gingerly and looked straight at

Jeanne. It has been almost five months since they saw each other. It felt awkward. Jock just stood there staring at Jeanne uncomfortably. Jeanne walked up to Jock and gave him a little kiss on his cheek. "I've missed you, Jock." Jock wrapped his arms around Jeanne and just held her for what seemed like an eternity without saying a word.

Jeanne pulled away from Jock but kept his hands with hers. "Come in Jock, mother is in the kitchen. She has been wondering when you were going to come around." With that, they walked into the house with Maggie trailing right behind. Jock looked around as they continued their walk down the main hallway, through the parlor and finally entering the kitchen located in the far back of the house.

June Daye was in the middle of frosting a cake she baked just a few hours before. Her baking skills were legendary among the neighborhoods. No matter what she baked whether it was carrot cake, cranberry bread, or her favorite custard pie, it always tasted like warm soft cardboard with a gritty topping of questionable ingredients. It was not one of her strong points. June was a tall woman, about 5 foot nine inches tall, the same height as her husband, but she was very slender, almost frail-like. Her hair was light brown and she liked to keep it shorter than what was considered the norm for that era. She wore glasses as thick as the bottom of a Coca-Cola bottle that made her look much older than she really was, but she needed them. She was blind as a bat.

"Hello, Jock," she said, looking up from the table where she was just finishing the final layer of frosting. She didn't know at the time but there was frosting in her hair and on the side of her face. Jeanne noticed right away and hastily helped her mother by wiping it off.

"Jeez, Mom," exclaimed Jeanne. "There is more frosting on you than there is on the cake."

"You wear it well, Mrs. Daye," responded Jock jokingly.

June was a little embarrassed but that didn't stop her from giving Jock a big hug. "Oh, Jock, it is so good to see you. We all missed you. How is your family? Are you home for good? Please have a seat. Can I get you a cup of tea?"

"No, no, thank you, Mrs. Daye. I just wanted to come over and tell everyone that I'm going into the Marine Corp. I passed the physical this time. I leave on November 3rd."

"Why that's only a few days from now," said a surprised Mrs. Daye as Jeanne stared into space.

Although Jeanne and Jock hadn't been dating since he left for Groton, Jeanne became very quiet and antsy. She started to tremble and then ran out of the room. "Jeez, I didn't think she would take it that bad," said Jock. "Well, you have to understand Jock; Jeanne has always held a special place in her heart for you. She saved all your letters. She will be all right, just give her a little time. She will come back in a minute or so. Now come over here and sit down, we have a lot of catching up to do."

As they were talking for what seemed like hours, Mr. Daye walked in. "Hello, Jock, what brings you around these parts? Where's Jeanne?" Just then, Jeanne walks down the back stairs into the kitchen greeting her father and then sitting down next to Jock. "Jock is going into the Marine Corp Daddy. He just came over to tell us."

"Well. then, this is a special occasion. Congratulation's, son," as Mr. Daye reached out to shake hands with Jock.

"Thank you, sir, I'm leaving in a couple of days so I thought I would come home and get things in order."

"Can you stay for dinner?" asked Mrs. Daye.

"No, ma'am, I really would like to take your daughter out, if that is all right with you both."

"It's fine with us," responded Mr. Daye. "Don't stay out too late and I hope we see more of you before you go."

"Yes. sir, I'll make it a point."

"Can I go too?" yelled Maggie.

"No... no, you stay here with us, you have homework to do, missy."

Jeanne ran back upstairs to get a sweater to wear under her coat. It was unseasonably cool this time of year in the evening. They walked back down to Union Square and stopped in at the local soda shop called Pews, which stood for Puritan's. Jock and Jeanne use to always frequent Pews with the rest of the gang. It was the best place in town to listen to music from the juke box and get triple chocolate frappes. Mr. Olson, the owner, always welcomed the kids. He would sit down with Jock and the others and just kid around. The best part of it was when Mr. Olson gave you a frappe for free on your birthday. It seemed like everybody had a birthday two or three times a year. Mr. Olson knew, but allowed it anyway.

Once inside, Jock put three nickels into the jukebox while Jeanne grabbed a vacant booth closer to the back where they could talk. As Jock turned away from the jukebox, he noticed Mr. Olson was not around. That's odd thought Jock; he practically lives behind those soda fountains. Walking over to the booth where Jeanne sat, he also noticed there were no familiar faces at the counter or at the booths. Sitting down opposite Jeanne he asked where Mr. Olson was. "Oh, didn't you hear? He died about a couple of months ago. He had a heart attack right here, behind the counter. It was awful. I think everybody in town went to the funeral. His son took over. You remember him, don't you?"

"How could I forget!" exclaimed Jock. "Sonny Olson was the one who taught me how to skate when I was five."

Sonny was about ten years older than Jock. He took him under his wing, sort of like a little brother.

A waitress came over to the booth. What will you two have said the waitress with a frazzled look on her face. "Two vanilla Cokes please... with no ice." The waitress looked down at them both with a little grin on her face. All right honey, two vanilla cokes coming right up... no ice!

When the waitress came back with the sodas, a man came out of the kitchen and spotted Jock instantly. "I thought it might be you," yelled the man with the apron tied around his waist.

"Hey, Sonny!" Jock got up and started over to the counter. Sonny walked around the counter with his uneven gait and firmly gripped Jock's hand. As a young child, Sonny was infected with Polio. "It's been a long... long time, how have you been?" asked Sonny.

"Swell, I just heard about your dad. I'm so sorry."

"Yeah, I was in the back room when it happened. Suddenly, I heard a commotion out front, some girls were screaming. When I got to him, he was already dead, a massive heart attack according to the doctor. He was sixty-five years old. He loved this joint. He loved all you kids coming in on Saturdays. We all miss him." There was a long pause then Sonny says, "As soon as I heard someone ordering vanilla Coke with no ice, I knew it had to be you."

"The Cokes are on me," said Sonny as the waitress came back with the sodas. "Thanks Sonny, but you don't have to."

"Sure, I do, you're a hockey legend around these parts."

"All because of you," said Jock. "If it wasn't for your encouragement, I probably would have ended up a juvenile delinquent or something."

"Nonsense; you were always the one who could see the forest through the trees. You were and always will be one of the good guys."

Jeanne just sat there listening intently as the two talked about old times. She really missed him these past five months. The waitress came back over to nudge Sonny a bit. Sonny realized that the shop was getting crowded, and he knew he had to get back into the kitchen to prepare all the orders that were piling up at the window between the counter and the kitchen.

"Okay... now it's just you and me," said Jeanne in a whisper. "I'm real glad you came to see me. I was wondering when we'd get to talk again."

"Yeah, I know what you mean. Well, at least we wrote to each other."

Jeanne gave a little sigh. "It's not the same, Jock. I'd rather talk than write to you every once in a while. So, are you seeing anyone?" asked Jeanne.

"No, I haven't found anyone that could light a candle to you. I guess you spoiled me," said Jock.

Now Jeanne was getting a little fidgety. "How about you?"

"No one on a regular basis. You know, maybe out to see a movie or down at Bruno's Bowling Alley."

"Bruno's! I thought you hated bowling," exclaimed Jock.

"Well, I'm not going to stay in all the time and become an old maid. I have a life too, you know!"

"Okay, okay, I'm sorry" (trying to calm the situation before she got too upset and walked out). "I know one thing. You probably have to swat the guys away."

"No, I don't have to do that," said Jeanne. "I just introduce them to my father. They never come back for a second date."

They both laughed. It was almost like the old days. Here in this soda shop with his best girl. *What could be better than this*, he thought to himself.

Jeanne looked up at the clock behind the counter. It was 9:45. "Oh my God! Look at the time! Would you take me home? I have to start work at six in the morning. I'm working a double shift tomorrow. There are not enough nurses, so many have gone over to England and Hawaii to help care for the wounded soldiers. I get paid well but the hours are killing me. I'm on my feet all day and night. By the time I get home, I'm just too tired to do much else but sleep."

"I understand, let's go. I'll walk you home."

Jeanne and Jock reached the steps to her home about 10:00 p.m. Jeanne leaned over to kiss Jock, and he wrapped his arms around her and kissed her back. "I had a wonderful time," said Jeanne.

"Me too. Can I see you tomorrow?"

A warm smile grew on Jeanne's face. "As long as you don't mind just sitting at home, I get out at 9:00 p.m. tomorrow. You can come over at 9:30 or so if you want."

"I don't mind at all," said Jock. "In fact, I'm looking forward to it." They kissed again and Jeanne walked into her home. "Good night, Jock."

Jock gave a little wave, "See you tomorrow."

The next morning Jock did not wake up until 9:00 a.m. When he got out of bed and showered, he walked downstairs but there was no one home. His sister Evelyn was already off to her job and little brother Bobby was probably lugging groceries all around town. Like Jock, Bobby was an avid hockey player and made the team his freshman year at Brighton High as well. Bobby looked up to his brother and emulated him in several ways. However, there was a difference between the two. Bobby was much more outgoing and gregarious while Jock was more of the quiet type. They were very close though and knew all they had was each other. Father had instilled that one good trait in his three children.

There was a note on the parlor room table that morning. It read that father was back down in Washington, DC and would not be home for a few more days. Uncle Tom and Aunts Lil and Peg were out of town visiting Tom's brother in Brookline, New Hampshire where he quarried granite for a living. Uncle Tom and his brother were craftsmen in stonework. Some of their finest work rested on top of many prominent family gravesites in the Greater Boston area including cornerstones in Copley Square.

After Nora passed away from tuberculosis, it was decided that Tom and Lil could provide their niece and nephews a more stable environment to grow up in than what William was able to provide. So, they moved back to the large, mansard style home on North Beacon Street to raise the three while William spent most of his time in Washington, DC.

Jock spent the day going through his things, baseball cards of his favorite players, a coin collection of silver dollars his dad helped him with, and a few photographs, some of which were of his mother and he as a toddler. Jock's heart was heavy with sadness. So many things in his life had gone terribly wrong. Starring at the photos Jock started to tremble uncontrollably. If only his mother was here, if only he was bigger, if only he was smarter. Jock calmed himself remembering what father used to say as they were growing up.

He would say, "If you think we have it bad, think of all those poor souls that have no home to call their own, who go to sleep hungry because their government is wrought with corruption, who don't have the opportunity to better themselves because they live in a place that doesn't allow you to keep the things you have earned and treasure the most. Yes, we are the blessed ones. We take too much for granted."

After reflecting, Jock continued sorting out his personal belongings to store in the attic. He would not need most of them now. All he needed basically were the clothes on his back and a few personal items such as the gold cross, a picture of his mother, and one other picture of his girl.

Chapter III

The Journey

November 3rd, 1942 would have been like any other day for Jock Donahoe only he wasn't in school or at work anymore. He was sitting in the back of the bus along with fifteen other young men headed for Springfield, Massachusetts. Once there they would pick up some other new recruits and continue to Trenton, New Jersey and then on to 30th Street Station in Philadelphia where they would change their mode of transportation to rail. The train would be completely full of men, all heading to the same destination—Parris Island, South Carolina. The train ride actually terminates in Florence, South Carolina where the recruits would undergo a final comprehensive medical evaluation and orientation before being transported by buses to Parris Island for six weeks of basic training.

Just before sunrise, Jock boarded the undistinguished grayish bus with dirty windows in Scollay Square. It was an unusually warm day. In fact, the past week felt more like September than November. Looking back to wave to his father, sister and brother for the last time sent a chill up Jock's spine even with the warm, sunny weather. He realized he may never see them again. The day before the whole family including his aunts, uncles and cousins got together at the house for a farewell party. Not surprisingly, Uncle Tom, as well as some of the other men had a little too much to drink.

His cousin, Jimmy Murphy, affectionately known as "Brother" was only eight and could not understand why all the women were crying and all the men laughing and talking aloud and patting Jock on the back. This was all too confusing for Jimmy, so he just kept to himself. At one-point Jock noticed young Jimmy sitting by himself in the corner of the parlor and went over to him.

"What's the matter?"

Jimmy, a little shy but who always warmed up to Jock asked quizzically, "Are you going to shoot Nazis?"

"No, I'm going to fight the Japanese and make sure they never attack this country again. Then, I'm gonna come home and take you fishing just like we did last year. Do you remember our fishing trip? You caught more fish than me. The next time I'm gonna beat you."

With that challenge, young Jimmy jumped up on the chair and says, "Uncle Jackie, you are a terrible fisherman; you didn't even catch one fish and I caught three! I betchya I will beat you again." And with that, they shook hands.

"You gotta deal," said Jock. "Now why don't you get some cake and ice cream and then go outside with the rest of your cousins and play kick the can?" Jimmy jumped off the chair and started walking toward the kitchen door to go outside.

He turned around and said, "I'm going to miss you, Cousin Jack. Please come home and don't get hurt."

"I promise," replied Jocko, holding back his emotions a bit, not wanting Jimmy to see, while looking out the window of the parlor where he could see the rest of his nieces and nephews playing outside.

Jock's thoughts are interrupted as the bus pulls to a stop at the Enlistment Center in Springfield. The rest of the day would entail waiting in different long lines, filling out forms, and another medical exam.

The following day, the newly enlisted Marine recruits load up on official Navy buses for a four-mile ride to the train terminal and board an awaiting train headed to Trenton, New Jersey. All Jock could smell was the acrid fragrance of diesel fuel emanating from the train's engine. Well at least he got a seat to himself where he could spread out till reaching Trenton.

Jock had never been farther than Groton, Connecticut before in his whole life so when the bus travelled through Groton, a little twinge of remorse crept into his mind. He shook it off and delved into the newspaper his dad gave him back at Scollay Square.

Arriving at their first destination in New Haven, Connecticut just after two in the afternoon, the eager recruits were allowed twenty minutes to hit the head or get coffee or whatever they wanted before the train rolled on. While sitting at the counter at the bus stop, he immediately noticed all the New York accents, and whispered to the guy on the stool to the left of him "Where did these folks learn to talk?" Not knowing that the guy he said it to was originally from White Plains, New York.

The guy turns to Jock and says, "I'd learn to keep my mouth shut if I were you." Jock realized that he might have stepped out of line, so he decided to heed the stranger's advice and finish his coffee in quiet.

The young man on the other side of Jock heard what he said and tapped Jock on the shoulder, "Hey, buddy, you should listen to the way you talk. I can tell you're from Boston." Jock spun around in his seat to size up his new opponent only to find that the new face was wearing a big grin and had extended his hand to introduce himself. "My name is Vincent DiNapoli, but you can call me Vin. All my friends do. I'm from the Bronx and I ain't got no accent."

Jock took the big guy's hand and firmly shook it wondering if he was the only one on the bus that did not talk funny. "My name is Donahoe, Jack Donahoe, but my friends call me Jock."

Vin replied, "So what do you want me call you, Jack or Jock?" Pausing for effect long enough for Vin's smile to disappear, Jock blurts out "I've got a funny feeling that you and I are going to be seeing a lot of each other, so call me Jock."

With that, Vin's grin returned even wider. "Wait until my mother finds out I have a harp as a new buddy."

"You think you got problems, responded Jock, wait till my old man finds out my new pal in the Corps is a wop." I can see the words forming on his lips "Jesus, Mary & Joseph, what is the world coming to!"

The two young men laughed so loud that the rest of the patrons just looked and shook their heads. They had at least twelve more hours to reach their final destination, and everybody was hoping to get some shuteye before the Drill Instructors down on Parris Island relieved them of that little privilege.

The train continued its journey down to Trenton, New Jersey. Jock could not help but think what lay ahead for him. This was the first time in his life that he was actually scared. A second cold shiver went down his spine and he had an uncontrollable shake that lasted all of a second, but it was enough for Vin to notice.

"Hey, if you're cold, man, I'm sure the stewardess can get you a blankie." Jock gave Vin that raised eyebrow look.

"Jeez, do you really think so? Perhaps she can tuck me in too!

Perhaps you should have gotten out of the Bronx more often cuz stewardesses are only on planes."

"You're a funny guy," said Vin. "So, what's a plane?"

"Never mind," Jock replied. "I can see that you're an uneducated fella. Looks like you're gonna need a lot of help. Stay close and learn from the master."

"Okay, Jock, as long as you don't get me killed."

"First things first," said Jock. "Let's get through basic training first."

Vin never let on to Jock that he was an exceptional student. He had been double promoted twice. Once from 5th to 7th grade, and the other from 9th to 11th grade. He was considered a genius with an IQ of 145. His mother and father were teachers. His dad was an English Professor at Trinity College, and his mom taught mathematics at the college also. Vin was always uncomfortable with this gift. He just wanted to be one of the guys. On many occasions, he would do poorly on a test just so people would not talk about him. The Marine Corps knew of his abilities but couldn't persuade him into entering the Naval Academy or even the Intelligence Sector. No, he wanted to be a Marine just like his older brother. Eventually, Vin would confide in Jock, at a time of his choosing.

Jock settled back into a more comfortable position but couldn't stop thinking about how he would react when he faced the enemy. Would he freeze the moment he saw action, or would he be one of the guys leading the charge? He guessed he would find out soon enough and then fell into a disconcerting sleep.

The brakes on the train squealed as it came to a stop into the terminal in Trenton at around 6:00 p.m. If the sharp shrill didn't wake everyone up the abrupt stop did. Everyone on the train needed to get out to stretch their legs and use the restroom at the terminal. The first thing Jock noticed was that this terminal must be brand new. There was a lot of chrome and the stools at the counter did not have the usual tears and frays like the ones back at Pew's. They also had his favorite drink on the menu, vanilla coke. As he orders his vanilla coke Vin could not help but overhear what Jock ordered. "Vanilla Coke!" Vin responds in a booming voice. "Why in God's green earth would anyone put vanilla in a perfectly good soda pop?"

Looking a little amused with his newly acquainted friend, Jock retorts, "Your girlfriend seemed to like it the other night." Vin was utterly speechless. He thought Jock was serious, but then realized he was snookered and began to get a little red in the face. "All right wise guy, you got me on that one. Just wait... payback's a bitch."

Before they could re-board, there was much commotion with train operators and other personnel walking up and down the entire length of the train looking for something. Then they got word this train wasn't going anywhere. That loud shrill heard earlier by everyone was caused by an axle breaking apart and scraping along the steel tracks. They had to wait five and a half hours at the terminal until substitute transportation could be arranged.

The revised mode of transportation turned out to be surplus school buses. Once boarded, they still had to wait to receive five additional recruits. All of them looked like they were still in high school except for the tall rangy kid with a scar on his left cheek that ran up to his hairline. He looked more like twenty-five and may have seen much of the world already. The other four youths seemed to hover around this guy, like they were his disciples or something. Jock figured that will change in an instant once they arrive at Parris Island.

The bus finally left the terminal and Jock could see a few women waving to their loved ones, perhaps for the very last time. At that moment, Jock felt very alone.

The steady drone of the bus engine slogging along at an even forty miles per hour acted like a hypnotic state for everyone on board. About 80 miles into this leg of the journey, Jock, and everybody else on the bus were suddenly woken by the loud screech and sudden shift in direction. Everything in the cargo shelf above their heads came crashing down on top of the young men. As Jock tried to brace himself, he saw one guy and some gear go right over his seat while at the same instant Jock found his face being introduced to the back of the seat in front of him.

Blood came squirting everywhere from his nose and mouth, he was quick enough to get his hands in front of him and grab the steel frame of the seat to lessen the full impact. Many of the others were not as lucky as they were completely caught unaware or were sleeping. The maneuver by the bus driver was just too severe. The bus came to a screeching halt in a ditch on the side of the road. It was dark and had started to rain. Everyone was in a state of confusion and a few profanities were bandied about.

The bus driver, a bit shaken, managed to call out to see if everyone was all right. He received mostly moans, groans, and some additional expletives. Assessing the carnage inside the bus, he sees that everyone is moving about trying to pick up their gear. Even the fella that flew over Jock's head managed to shake it off. It appeared that Jock got the worst of it, nothing broken, just blood all over his shirt.

"What a way to start basic training," yelled Vin. "What are they trying to do, kill us before the Japs can?"

The bus driver and the recruits got off the bus to see what happened and are greeted with the mangled caucus of a deer and the still smoking right front tire as flat as a pancake. To make matters worse, the bus had careened into a ditch that was three feet deep and full of water and mud. It would take all the recruits two hours to get it back on the pavement with a spare tire in place. By the time the bus was ready to continue its trek, all the wannabe Marines were soaked to the skin. The good news was the bleeding had stop from Jock's nose. "Oh well, so much for any sleep," Jock said sarcastically to anyone within earshot. There were a couple of muffled retorts.

The squeal of the brakes as it pulled into the 30th Street train terminal in Philly was a welcome sound this time. Their entertaining bus ride was over and now perhaps they would be able to rest a little more comfortably in a passenger cab of the train heading directly to Florence, South Carolina.

Jock and Vinnie got seats in the first row and were sound asleep before the train left the station. Their clothes were still wet and muddy, but that didn't matter. Sleep mattered.

Arriving in Florence, the recruits were able to disembark and stretch their legs. They even had time to make any last-minute calls if they were quick enough to get over to the few phone booths situated just outside the terminal. Looking over at the long line forming at the booths, Jock and Vinnie decided to nix that idea and headed inside to the news stand and peruse the headlines on the newspapers until the salesclerk yelled at them to either buy one or get out.

Twenty minutes later their convoy of vehicles pulled up in front of the station for their final leg. These last few hours of transport were going to be the worst as the only mode of transportation that could be conjured up were dilapidated Greyhound buses dating back to the 1920s. which had been given little to no maintenance since then. An eerie silence fell over all the occupants.

The busloads of disheveled recruits finally made it to the gates of Parris Island just before midnight on November 5th. Once inside the depot, the recruits disembarked from the convoy and were instructed by a junior drill instructor to line up on the painted yellow footprints. After calling out their names, the junior drill instructor along with two MPs rustled them over to the Receiving building where they could make a single telephone call to let their loved ones know they arrived safely. Then they were made to give up any non-essential personal effects; issued some military clothing and start the long process of filling out forms. Once they completed these tasks, they were led over to the Squad Bay for some shuteye before reveille. Shuteye would not come for most.

Chapter IV

Indoctrination

It was still pitch black out when they heard the bugle call. It seemed like they had just got in their racks fifteen minutes ago. Now this awful earsplitting sound and two very loud instructors kicking each rack and screaming profanities were rousting them as they made their way down the tightly spaced rows of bunks.

The new recruits staggered and collided into one another trying to react to their new environment. Jock could not help cracking a grin while thinking to himself that this was going to be hell.

Gathered out in front of their Squad Bay, an extremely agitated and threatening voice boomed from somewhere behind Jock. A small but stocky man with the face of a Pit Bull strutted around the unorganized and sleep-deprived crowd. Accompanying this man on both sides of him were two much larger men. Both had MP insignias on their armbands and helmets. It didn't take long for everyone to see that this was not going to be a pleasant day.

The man in charge just looked at the scene in front of him. Pausing until everyone could plainly see that he was not a happy person. Silence immediately overcame the crowd. That was when Sergeant-Major Hank Gustafson barked out his welcome speech.

"Good morning, ladies and welcome to the United States Marine Corps Recruiting Depot, Parris Island, South Carolina. You are now property of the 2nd Marine Division. I hope your trip was enjoyable. Because that is the last damn thing you all are going to enjoy until this Godforsaken war is over! This next six weeks are going to make you into United States Marines so help me God. You will be feared by the enemy, envied by our brothers in arms and respected by the rest of the world. You will be worked until you don't think you can take anymore, (pausing for effect) but you will. Because there are only two ways off this island… a pine box or a Greyhound bus."

The sergeant major continued with his prepared speech that he has spewed out since the Japs bombed Pearl Harbor. "My name is

Sergeant Major Gustafson. My job is to give you the tools and the training to defeat any enemy, secure any beachhead, and protect America's interests at home or abroad. You will defend our nation from all enemies, near or far. You will be molded into the finest soldiers ever to walk the face of this earth."

"This is going to be accomplished by me kicking your ass all over this little camp of ours. Sergeant Shields to my right and Sergeant Mace to my left are my junior drill instructors and will assist in fulfilling this objective. You will become the toughest, meanest, scariest sons of bitches to ever wear a United States uniform. You will be United States Marines. You will be the best."

"Now that you are all rested, you will follow the sergeants and double time it to Building H where you will be issued the remaining necessary articles of clothing and supplies you will be responsible for the duration of your enlistment. Sergeant Shields, they are all yours."

As Sergeant Shields began to bark out his own message to the recruits, Jock could not help but feel a surge of pride but also intimidation to what was about to unfold. He noticed the grin on Vin's face disappear as they high tailed it over to Building H. It was about 5:30 AM and glimpses of sun light were just starting to peak through the hickory trees that lined the main entrance to the camp. A chill in the air left the recruits with a vapor trail rising over each figure from their heavy breathing.

By the time, the seventy-four recruits received their gear it was nearly 0700 hours. All of them were famished. Vinnie, weighing about 205 pounds was keenly aware of his lack of sustenance and made no bones about his irritation. "Hey Sarge, when do we eat?"

Sergeant Shields took one look at him and walked over to the door leading to the mess hall. "You eat when I tell you to eat. But right now, I'm telling you bunch of lily-asses to get your gear over to your assigned barracks and muster out front in five minutes. Then we are going to have a little run... about a 5-mile run. After that you can eat. Now move it you bunch of mammas boys."

About halfway through the run, Jock's side began to cramp. He started to slow down to see if the pain would subside but all it did was make it worse. Jock knew if he didn't finish this run, the sergeant would make his next six weeks worse than a living hell. So, he went on, through the pain and all, trying anyway he could to ignore the signals telling him to stop and rest. Four of the other recruits already succumbed to the humidity. Some water and a long walk back to the barracks were what awaited them. Tomorrow would be more difficult for those who could not finish this first test of endurance. Tomorrow would come all too soon for the entire group.

At about the 4-mile point, two more recruits dropped out. They too would be dealt with the same intensity and manner as the ones that fell out earlier. There were no favorites in the Marine Corps. Jock's cramps seemed to be waning. He looked around to the rear and could see Vinnie laboring to keep up with the group. With that, Jock purposely slowed down for Vinnie to catch up. With only a half mile to go, Jock reached over and smacked Vinnie in the arm. With a quizzical expression, Vinnie laboriously called out "What did you do that for?" Jock responded by accelerating ahead. He was hoping Vinnie would follow suit. He did. Soon Jock and Vinnie were passing the remainder of the recruits. Not to be out done, several of the others gave chase. But nobody in the group could catch Jock, except the sergeant. Sergeant Shields matched Jock's stride pace for pace without breaking a sweat. Within one hundred feet of the finish line, Sergeant Shields simply left Jock in a cloud of dust.

Jock waited for the others in front of the barracks. The other junior drill instructor was only a few seconds behind and gave Jock an evil glance as he approached. A few of the wiry guys came next. Then Vin huffing and puffing. Instead of running by Jock, he ran into him knocking Jock flat on his ass.

"Jeez Jock, I'm really sorry. I didn't think—" but before Vin could finish, Sergeant Shields was all over him. "So, you think you can throw your weight around, maggot! Let's see you try that again, this time on me."

By then Jock was able to recover from the blow he received and interjected. "Sergeant Shields, it was my doing. I instigated him during the run. He was only paying me back, that's all."

The sergeant was not one for missing an opportunity, so he decided to have a little fun at their expense. "All right, then, in a couple of days, you two are going to put on an exhibition match for us all. However, for right now everybody reports back to their barracks for inspection. The mess hall closes in twenty minutes, so I suggest that you maggots double-time it if you want to eat. Now move it!"

Five minutes later the new recruits eagerly had lined up at the mess hall waiting in turn to receive their plateful of a hot, gooey substance. Upon closer inspection each serving looked like a soft lump of light brown slime on a graham cracker. Whatever it was the Marines stuffed their faces with it. Most of them didn't know what they were eating but it did not matter at the moment. A couple of the guys ate so fast that they regurgitated it back up. Their bodies were not use to the extreme physical workout they just received after the long and sleepless bus ride. Unfortunately, one of the vomiting recruits was sitting next to Jock and opposite Vin.

"Oh jeezuz!" yelled Vin. Jock was quick enough to grab his plate and turn the other way as the guy emptied the contents of his gut on the table. Vin was not as lucky sitting directly opposite the guy. The rest of the guys at the table laughed as Vinnie got sprayed. "I'm sorry man" said the pale-faced recruit to Vin. "I couldn't control it. I'm sorry." Vin realized the poor guy was as sick as a dog and did not seek revenge. "Good shot pal," muttered Vin. "Next time; aim at the guy next to you." Jock couldn't help but smirk at the whole ordeal. At that point, nobody was hungry anymore. All they could think of was what Sergeant Shields had planned for them after breakfast.

By the time the two sick recruits and Vin were cleaned up it was 0800 hours, Sergeant Shields and his aides were just finishing inspecting everyone's military garb and bunks. The squad was rather proud of themselves with their new combat fatigues and boots. The Drill Sergeant was not that impressed though. He immediately got into several of the recruits' faces, chewing them out one by one until his voice got hoarse.

"All right you scum buckets, now that you all look dapper with your shiny new boots, lets break them in with another 5-mile run."

Halfway through the run the Drill Instructors decided to have a little fun with them. "Marines, halt! Drop and give me fifty and call them out in unison." The platoon obliged and jumped back up to attention. "You call those pushups? Give me fifty more!" the Marines try again but most struggled to get past twenty. Sergeant Mace screams at the top of his lungs. "You call yourselves Marines? I call you candy-asses! Get back up in formation and start running." The men get back into rhythm when the Drill Instructors blow their whistles again. Just ahead are a series of wood poles standing about 30 feet high. Marines! First man to make it to the top does not have to run the remaining miles. After about ten minutes, only eight could reach the top. Jock was among those but not the first.

There is a slight devious grin on Mace's face. "You sorry sonsofbitches! My seventy-five-year-old grandmother could do better than most of you. Get back into formation and double time it back to camp."

Most of the Marines were dragging their asses rounding the corner to the camp. Jock chose to run the rest of the way with the men but stayed near the rear. This way he at least kept up with the main pack but was able to keep an eye on Vinnie trailing far behind. Vinnie was in with a small pack of stragglers that got back to camp last and was then chewed out by Mace for no other apparent reason than he just did not like him.

After the chewing out, Jock walked over to Vinnie and immediately notice his left hand was bleeding. A closer look revealed he had a 2-inch splinter of wood in the palm of his hand. "We gotta get you to the infirmary Vinnie to get that looked at and dressed before it gets infected" Grimacing in pain, Vinnie concedes to their advice but before heading to the infirmary, Mace walks over to find out what the problem was. He notices the bleeding hand and says, "Good thing it's your left hand DiNapoli. You can shoot with your right." Vinnie wanted to knock his block off or at least tell him where to go but decided to bite his lip, for now.

The wound needed a few stitches. Vinnie grimaced as they worked on his hand and then got bandaged up. He was almost as good as new just before noon. At least he would not miss chow.

After chow, the recruits were issued their brand-new Garand M-1 rifles and bayonets. The M-1 had just become the new "standard issue for all US Forces replacing the venerable Springfield bolt action rifle used during WW I. The M-1 was a true semi- automatic gas operated rifle using a .30-caliber magazine. No ammunition was passed out knowing damn well someone could blow their head off before they got to the firing range. A young-looking instructor had the entire squad sit on the ground while he introduced the basic parts of this fine instrument of death. He even demonstrated with uncanny precision how to disassemble all the parts of the rifle and put the pieces back together while the squad gawked in awe. When it was their turn to try, not a single one of them could take apart and put back together their rifle without dropping a piece in the process. So, they stayed for hours and hours until every single one of them got the ritual done in less than a minute. Jock and Vinnie were among the first to master this technique. The remaining portion of the day consisted of calisthenics, climbing rope, crawling through mud and push-ups... lots of push-ups.

That evening, Jock got to know and make friends with some of the other guys. Charlie Azuroni was from Meridian, Connecticut. His dad owned a car dealership, and he told his new acquaintances that after the war they could get a new Ford at his dad's cost. Jock and Vinnie decided to give him the nickname Chaz, and it stuck. Sam Walker was from East Cranston, Rhode Island.

Sam was from a long tradition of Marines in his family. He was only seventeen and looked even younger, but he got kicked out of high school because of lighting a fire in the girls' locker room of their archrival Lasalle High School just before a big football game.

All four of them made a pledge and formed a pact that they would look out for each other through boot camp and onto war if they were lucky enough to stay together. The barrack lights went out at 2100 hours. They all anticipated hell was coming for them for the next six weeks. They would not be disappointed. The entire contingent fell asleep within ten minutes of crashing on their bunks.

Reveille was called at 0500 the next morning. Some of the guys fell out of their bunks in complete and utter disarray while others did not even stir. It was these late risers that received Sergeant Shields complete and undivided wrath. Anyone still in their bunk by the time Sergeant Shields entered the Quonset hut learned just how hard the floor was.

Sergeant Shields had a small squad of MPs with him as he scouted the number of bunks that were still occupied and had two MP's lift one side of each bunk spilling its contents with a loud *thunk*.

Of the seventy-four recruits in this company, five of them were made to clean the latrine with toothbrushes while still in their shorts. The remaining recruits completed their paperwork over in Building H.

By 0700 hours, the entire group gathered back in front of their Quonset hut and were split into two platoons of thirty-seven each. Jock and Vin were lucky enough to be in the same platoon with Drill Instructor Sergeant Shields. Chaz and Sam were in the other platoon.

Sergeant Shields was from Braintree, Massachusetts. He had been in the Marine Corps for eleven years right out of high school. His aim was to get this latest group of raw recruits through boot camp and then his third tour of duty would be just about up. He would go back home to college to become a teacher. He loved math and the sciences and hoped to teach at the high school level once out of college. What Sergeant Shields didn't realize was his country would call him for a higher mission, a mission to lead this particular group to war.

There was something about Sergeant Shields that Jock liked. He could not put his finger on it, but he had a gut feeling that this guy was going to make him into the best of the best. Jock was ready.

As the recruits stood at attention in the cold, damp and windy morning, Sergeant Shields ordered both platoons over to the training arena just beyond the obstacle course. He then instructed Jock and Vin to put on some protective headgear and pick up the Pugil Sticks. Neither one of them knew what the heck pugil sticks were, so the sergeant picked up one of the pugil sticks and performed a quick demonstration with one of the other junior drill instructors. After about two minutes of instruction, Jock and Vin entered the improvised ring and faced each other.

"On the whistle, I want you two to battle. The first man that goes down loses," said Sergeant Shields. Vin and Jock just looked at each other, a little intimidated at first, but that disappeared as soon as the whistle blew.

Vin took the first swing at Jock even before the whistle stopped screeching and hit Jock right off the side of his head. Jock was able to recover and stepped back just in time for what would have been a crushing blow to the other side of his head. As soon as the end of the padded pugil stick went whizzing by, Jock jabbed his pugil stick right in Vin's face knocking him back a couple of feet. Blood was running down Vin's face. He tried to wipe it off but was greeted with another butt to the stomach. The blows that Jock was inflicting were more of a nuisance to the big guy. Jock stood ready for Vin's counter assault. When it came, it was overwhelming. Vin charged straight at Jock swinging the stick as fast and hard as he could. Jock was able to deflect the first two swings but could not stave off the onslaught. Vin's third thrust hit Jock squarely in the chest. The wind was knocked out of Jock, and he went down on one knee... but was not out. As Vin came in for the final blow, Jock mustered all his remaining strength and rammed the pugil stick square into Vin's balls. Vin went down like a sack of potatoes and turned two shades of purple. Jock tried to get up but fell to both knees and then keeled over. The match was over. Sergeant Shields ruled it a draw and had two of the recruits take the two battered warriors to the infirmary where ice would be dispensed.

"You're one tough bastard," whispered Vin still not fully recovered from Jock's last strike. "And you sure can take a hit," said Jock. "You swatted my hardest hits like flies! I'm sorry I had to resort to hitting you in the nuts, but not that sorry. I was more afraid of what you were about to do to me."

"I learned one thing today," said Vin.

"When bullets start flying, you're the one I want to share a foxhole with covering my backside."

"Thanks Vin, the same goes for me."

Leaving the infirmary, the two walked gingerly back over to the pugil stick demonstration which was still going on. As soon as Sergeant Shields noticed them from the corner of his eye, he motioned them over to him. "I see you two maggots are feeling better now. Now get back out there and practice." This went on until 1000 hours and then the squad double-timed it to the agility course.

"All right, you maggots, listen up," roared Sergeant Shields. "Sergeant Mace is going to lead off. You are to follow him for the entire course. If any one of you slacks off or falls behind or misses any of the stations, I'm gonna personally rip you a new asshole! Is that understood?" The squad replied in a meek "Yes, sir."

"I can't hear you," roared the sergeant again, and again the squad elevated their voices in the affirmative. "I still can't hear you!" bellowing from the top of his lungs.

"Yes, sir!!" came the sharp and highly audible response.

"Sergeant Mace, get these maggots out of my sight."

Three weeks into boot camp the group of recruits were looking more and more like United States Marines. They were acting as a unit. One mindset, one objective, and one purpose, to kick the Japanese all the way back to Tokyo and making sure they never make the same mistake twice – sneak attack on US soil. Even the superior officers were starting to see the progress of the Master Sergeants methods.

Master Sergeant Gustafson along with Drill Instructor Shields and Junior Drill Instructor Mace were back in their Quonset hut preparing for the next day's training. It was 1900 hours and the sun had shone its last rays for that day one half hour ago. Everything was peaceful, almost too much so. Not even the buzz of mosquitos or the shrill of crickets were in the air. Instructor Mace commented first. "Doesn't that make your skin crawl when there is complete silence?"

"It reminds me of the calm before the storm," echoed Master Sergeant Gustafson.

"That's what I'm afraid of," said Mace. "I'm just not sure we can get these recruits ready in six short weeks... so many of these kids have never held a rifle in their hands before and we are trying to make them into simple killing machines, ready to march into harm's way when ordered."

Looking directly into Instructor Mace's eyes, Sergeant Shields said in a sullen tone, "That's our job. We can only prepare them the best we know how and pray to God it is good enough."

"Amen to that," replied Master Sergeant Gustafson. "Amen to that."

Chapter V

The Making of a Marine

Daily rifle practice had honed the recruits' marksmanship ability to near perfection apart from a few that just could not make the grade. It seemed Vin was having the most difficulty. No matter what position he tried, whether it was prone or in the basic kneeling position, Vin had this nasty habit of closing his eyes each time he squeezed the trigger. This led to missing the target completely on several occasions. Even the Drill Instructors could not break Vin of this habit. The test for a marksman was to be held this Saturday, only three days away. If he did not pass, he would be transferred to a non-combative position. Vin could not bear for this to happen. With just over one week left of Boot Camp, Vin was desperate to overcome his disability.

Meanwhile, Jock was busy trying to design a device that could be placed around Vin's eye, sort of like a monocle that would prevent Vin from closing his eye during the test. Jock had carefully sketched up a design and brought it over to the Corps machine shop where the machinist could hopefully fabricate this unique eyepiece.

Friday evening, Jock and Vin walked over to the machine shop after chow. When they got to within one hundred feet of the shop, they both noticed Sergeant Shields was already there talking to the machinist that had fabricated the device. Vin and Jock looked at each other with knots in their stomach.

"Oh shit," muttered Vin. "It looks like the jig is up."

"Not so fast, Vin. Let's give the sarge some leeway. Just don't say a word. Let me do the talking," Jock said discreetly.

As they walked through the large bay door, Sergeant Shields turned around to greet them. "DiNapoli, Donahoe, what brings you two into my world this evening?" Vin just stood there looking at Jock, then Jock addressed the sergeant. "Good evening, Sergeant Shields, we... err.... well, we came over to pick up Vin's belt buckle... . That's right, the buckle that was issued to him snapped in half, so this good man here was kind enough to make him a new one." The machinist dropped the cigar from his mouth and just looked at Jock in total confusion. Sergeant Shields caught the machinist's expression out of the corner of his eye but decided not to pursue it any further. He knew something was up, and he knew it probably had to do with the marksmanship test tomorrow morning. "Is that so?" responded the sergeant. "Well, then, you gentlemen get your asses back to your squad bay after you complete this little mission so you can rest up for tomorrow's activities."

"Yes, sir," they replied in unison.

Once Shields moved on to more important business, the machinist pulled out something out of his pocket that resembled a hollow copper ring the size of a half-dollar with smooth rounded edges and a flared bottom so the piece would rest on his cheekbone. There was no inner glass as all the device needed to do was to keep Vin's eye from closing when pulling the trigger. On their way back to the barracks Vin would try to keep it from falling off by squinting. It did fall off a couple of times, but Vin caught it before it hit the ground.

Back in their squad bay, Vin tells the story to the rest of the guys. None of them would believe it. They knew Sergeant Shields wouldn't give anybody an inch, especially his so called "Pain in the Asses" twosome. Jock and Vin seemed to always be on the Sarge's shit list for one thing or another. One night after "lights out," Jock and Vin snuck out of their squad bay to go swimming. Although it was the end of November and the air outside was a brisk 50 degrees, Vin dared Jock to the scheme, so Jock really did not have any choice. As they were coming out from the surf, they were greeted by Sergeant Shields and two MP's which threw them into the brig for the evening only wearing their soaking undershorts. The next morning, they had to lead the entire squad for a six-mile run with all their gear. Vin and Jock were still in their undershorts and bare feet for the entire run.

Jock had this rather good knack at drawing caricatures. He had sketched up Sergeant Major Gustafson with an oversized head and undersized body giving orders to Sergeant Shields and Mace as to how to run the outfit. The rendering looked like it could have come right out of the cartoon section of a major newspaper. Unfortunately, someone had retrieved it from under Jock's bunk and posted it on the bulletin board at the mess hall where all could see. Jock knew he should have never put his initials on that sketch.

But with all the idiotic things that Vin and Jock were caught doing, it did not seem to affect Sergeant Shields. In fact, after a while, he took a liking to both. Moreover, in many instances he just looked the other way. He knew these two had what it takes to be good Marines. Although a little unorthodox, they were tough and would go through hell and back to make the sergeant proud.

At 0515 hours on Saturday, the platoon woke to their ritualistic lifestyle of reveille and inspection. By 0630 hours, the platoons had taken their positions at the range and ready to commence firing when ordered with the hope of receiving their marksmanship medals.

Jock, Chaz, and Sam got perfect scores and received the rating of expert with the M-1 rifle. When it came time for Vin's turn the entire platoon seemed to turn their heads in his direction to see the outcome. Vin did not disappoint. He hit the target every time. Maybe not within the circles on each shot, but good enough to pass. The squad let out a roar. As soon as Vin got up from the prone position, he let the monocle slip into his shirt pocket before he turned around to face Sergeant Mace. "Good job, Marine," barked Sergeant Mace. "I wasn't sure you were gonna make it. Outstanding."

That evening, everyone in the barracks was in good spirits. Of the seventy-four recruits going into boot camp, there were only sixty-two left and they still had one more week of training. Of the sixty-two, four were in the sick ward for various ailments. The guys got to watch a movie over at the PX and play some pool. By 2000 hours they were all back at squad bay preparing their gear and weapons for tomorrow's mock battle to be orchestrated out on the southern quadrant of the base. Instead of packing their new M-1's, they would be issued wooden replicas of the old tried and true Deerfield rifles used during World War One. They would also be issued two smoke grenades each.

The recruits were greeted to an earlier than usual morning wake-up. A light drizzle encompassed the entire horizon as they received their final briefing and went through their formalities gearing up for today's exercises.

The platoons were designated Teams Alpha and Bravo. Team Alpha would conduct the main offensive operations against the camp. Team Bravo would have two missions. The first would be to reinforce Alpha in the event their casualties sustained too high of losses and were unable to continue the operation on their own. The second objective would be to initiate a mortar salvo and create a diversion to attract the enemy scouts away from Team Alpha, while not allowing them to get too close discovering the real intent. The war game rested in the middle of eight-hundred acres of woodlands and swamp.

Team Alpha's direct mission was to penetrate the base, neutralize as many of the enemy as possible, extract nine POWs, and take the base commander as a prisoner. They were given a layout of the camp and some rough estimates on the opposition's size and strength. The rest would be up to the platoon's leaders as to when and how they would complete the mission, so long as it was conducted within the next twenty-four hours. Judges would be placed among each platoon to decide who killed who during engagements. The engagement would be called Operation Moonlight Serenade.

In an unorthodox doctrine, Lieutenant Blaine instructed Second Lieutenant Bates to delegate one platoon to Sergeant Shields and another to Sergeant Mace. He wanted to see their capabilities in the event a real-life situation occurred, and their superior officer was incapacitated.

So, the two sergeants with twenty-nine grunts each moved into the deep woods in the direction of the purported enemy camp one-hour before sunrise. They wanted to be within striking distance by the time daylight broke. Their revised game plan was to set up a diversion force some four-hundred yards southwest of the camp. One third of this force would slip back another fifty yards to the west to set up mortar positions. Another one third would protect their northern flank and reinforce Team Alpha when called upon. The remaining one third would charge toward the camp then stop within one hundred yards and disperse and cover trying to draw the camp's forces out from their positions and into the line of fire of the mortars. The mortar squad would use blue smoke rounds.

Once everyone was in position, Sergeant Mace would orchestrate the diversion from the observation post on Hill 21 by two-way radio.

The remaining soldiers commanded by Sergeant Shields would infiltrate from the north. They would break up into two squads. Jock would lead squad one. His objective was to take out any outposts as quietly as possible. His men would spread out to approximately twenty yards apart from each other and use the rubber bayonets on their mock rifles to subdue the enemy.

Sergeant Shields would then take the remaining force through the cleared zone, enter the camp, and finish off the force guarding the POWs. With any luck, they would also be able to capture some of the enemy including their commander.

As the diversion force commenced operations, Sergeant Mace had a semi-clear field of view of the events unfolding since leaves had fallen from the unseasonably cool weather over the last week.

The enemy took the bait and committed half of their force to the diversion. As soon as the enemy force entered the field of fire for the mortar squad, Sergeant Mace cued Jock to engage.

The first phase of Operation Moonlight Serenade went off without a hitch. The judges ruled that the camp's team that entered the killing zone of the mortar squad were effectively out of action with eighty percent casualties.

Phase Two did not go as well. Over forty percent of Jock's squad got bushwhacked as soon as they started their infiltration. It seems that the Camp's forces designated as Team Charlie was anticipating a similar maneuver and had set up a trap, By the time the outposts were taken out, there was only Jock and seven others left from his squad. But it also left only a token force guarding the POWs. In addition, their commander was still in the camp with minimal protection. This gave Sergeant Shields with his remaining squad an excellent opportunity to complete his mission.

The camp layout had the nine voluntary POWs in an outdoor stockade in the center of the camp. There was one watchtower with two guards just to the east of the stockade. The watchtower was equipped with a wooden machine gun mock-up. The barracks and commander's hooch were situated on the far western side of the camp.

While Team Bravo's mortar squad held the remaining survivors of the initial diversion captive, elements of Bravo's diversion squad proceeded to the camp to draw fire from the guard post. Then Sergeant Shields pushed forward right up the middle while Jock and his small band would lob their improvised grenades up into the guard tower and run for cover. The only unknown was if there were any mines sewn in the open area between the outposts and the watchtower. They got their answer when two of Jock's remaining forces walked into some trip wires setting off plumes of red smoke as they dashed across the field reducing thus their ranks down to five.

The guards in the watchtower still had the original and larger threat to their southern and western flanks and could not redirect their fire on Jock and the other four until it was too late. Jock's first lob hit the roof of the tower but fell harmlessly to the ground.

"What the hell?" just then realizing he forgot to light it. Furiously he found his zippo and lit his last one. This time he threw it with no arc, and it landed directly between the three enemy men handling the gun emplacement. A second later, another smoke bomb found its mark. The watchtower was out of commission.

"Hey, Donahoe. I hear the Sox are looking for a relief pitcher," someone yelled out.

Like a well-executed stage performance by the Rockettes, Sergeant Shields directed his squad to storm in full force the commander's quarters and the remaining enemy guarding the stockade. The first one into the Commander's hooch was Vin. As he charged through the door, he crouched low and rolled head over heal until he landed clear across the other side of the small quarters. The camp commander tried to get a bead on Vin with his mock pistol but was greeted with two rifles pointed right at him, courtesy of Jock and Sam. As Vin got up to brush himself off, Sergeant Shields entered the hooch and saluted the Camp Commander... Master Sergeant Hank Gustafson.

"Well done, Sergeant. Your men are to be commended," bellowed the Master Sergeant. "Thank you, Sir. The men adapted, improvised, and executed the plan like a well-oiled machine," responded Sergeant Shields with a little more than just a grin on his face. "Let us hope they perform this well under real battle conditions... when blood is spilled," retorted Gustafson.

The final casualty count for the operation was Alpha Team with fourteen dead and six wounded; Bravo Team with three dead and four wounded, and the enemy designated as Camp Force Charlie who suffered twenty-six dead, five wounded, and eight captives not including the Base Commander. The nine freed POWs suffered no casualties. Of all the platoons on the base during this six-week training regiment, Sergeant Shields' platoon that Lieutenant Blaine delegated to him took first in this exercise.

The Marines in the truck with Jock and his buddies were in rather good spirits on the ride back to camp. Most were boasting of their success with securing their objectives. Even Vinnie joined in with the patting of backs. Jock just sat back, content with not screwing up.

During the ride back to their squad bay, the troops broke into the Battle Hymn of the United States Marine Corps.

Chapter VI

West Coast Transit

Preparations for their next adventure were underway. The sixth and final week at Parris Island would be completed tomorrow, December 18th, ending with a small ceremony confirming the recruits as full-fledged Marines. They would be issued their official ranks as privates. Their official designation was Unit 1280, 3rd Battalion, 6th Marines, Companies F, G, H, and I, of the 2nd Marine Division although some of the men would be transitioned into other battalions and even other regiments once they arrived in San Diego.

Most of this battalion, some three hundred and sixty men, would be transferred via air transports to San Diego, California for further instruction on amphibious warfare techniques. They would also be integrated into a larger fighting force comprised of a regiment consisting of several replacement battalions. This training would last for two weeks and then on to fight the Japanese wherever Uncle Sam instructed them to go.

That evening Jock wrote letters home to his family and Jeanne. All he could tell them was that he was on his way to the west coast. His letter to Jeanne was filled with emotion and sincerity and went like this:

Dear Jeanne,
I hope everyone is well in your family. Please give my regards to your mom and dad, and don't forget little Maggie too. If she turns out to be half as beautiful as you, she is going to have a difficult time keeping the guys away. These last six weeks got me to think of what a wonderful gal you are and that I must have been crazy to leave you to work at Pratt and Whitney. I hope you will forgive me. I will always hold those swell times that we had close to my heart. Maybe when I come home, I can take you bowling! Only kidding. Anyway, It's official, I'm a private in the US Marine Corp now. We just got orders we are shipping out to the west coast. They say that it is beautiful out there and I only wish we could see it to-

gether. I'm still with my same good buddies. They are a swell bunch of guys. We all look out for one another. When I showed them your picture, they all hooted and hollered. They couldn't figure out why a classy dame like you would stick with a guy like me. I told them that you like my single eyebrow. That's about it for now. I will write to you as soon as I can. I have a funny feeling that we will not be there for long. Well, I have to go. The Marine Corps is all about hurry up and wait. This much I can tell you, you are my best girl and I hope you will wait for me to come home. We are going to send the enemy back across the Pacific with their tails between their legs. This I promise you. Say a prayer for us. God Bless kiddo.
Jock

The rest of his platoon was doing the exact same thing, writing to family and loved ones. It was so quiet in the squad bay because everyone was so focused on finishing their letters. Nobody even noticed Sergeant Shields and Sergeant Mace had entered the quarters for at least thirty seconds. When one of the guys did look up, he hollered "Ten Hut." The entire platoon jumped to their feet at attention.

"At ease Marines," came the melancholy reply from Sergeant Shields. "I've got good news and bad news for you. The good news is you won't have Sergeant Mace in your face any more like the last six weeks. The bad news is: I'm going with you to amphibious assault training in San Diego." The Marines let out a cheer in unison, then all was silent. "At 0600 hours tomorrow, we will be boarding Douglas DC-3s from our base to San Diego. Make sure you bring only what was instructed to bring. If I find anyone of you maggots packing anything else that was not authorized, I will personally kick your butt out of the plane at 14,000 feet without a parachute. Is that understood!" Sgt. Mace turned one hundred and eighty degrees and exited the squad bay in precise military fashion.

Saturday, December 20th, at 0600 hours the eight platoons of Marines boarded the ten DC-3s that already had their engines revving on the tarmac. Jock and Vin sat beside each other along the outer wall of the fuselage. Sam and Chaz sat across the bay. Sergeant Shields had a more strategic but no more comfortable seat just aft of the flight crew's cabin. From that location he could look all the way down the fuselage to keep an eye on his men. This was the first time for many of the Marines to be on a plane. Some were excited. The quiet ones not so. Jock wondered how this big bird could lift all these men with their heavy equipment off the ground and stay up without spiraling out of control back down to earth. It fascinated him.

The plane lifted off from the tarmac. Vin clenched his fists. Jock could see that Vin was not an avid fan of having nothing but air between him and the earth. Jock offered Vin a stick of gum, but Vin had his eyes closed. It looked to Jock that he was praying.

Sweat started to form on Vin's face. "Relax," said Jock. "If the good Lord wants you there is nothing you can do about it." Vin finally opened his eyes and said, "If the good Lord wants me dead, now would be as good a time as any." Some of the other guys heard Vin. It seemed to release some of the tension that was on the plane.

Their first layover for refueling was just on the outskirts of Oklahoma City. The pilot hit the gravel airstrip a little too hard and the plane bounced back up in the air roughly twenty feet leaving most of the men's stomachs on the ground while the rest of their bodies followed suit with the plane. Vin was taken by complete surprise the most, and clutched onto Jock's shoulder digging his fingernails deep in. All Jock could do was grimace and hope the pilot would get this contraption down on the ground pronto. The pilot managed to make the necessary corrections and within a few seconds, the plane was taxiing to the disembarking point. Vin did not waste any time getting off the plane. By the time Jock got off, Vin's complexion returned to a normal state instead of the pale white complexion he had all the way from Parris Island.

Refueling would take about one-half hour, so the Marines got to stretch their legs in the cool morning sun. When the plane was fully fueled, it took all the courage Vin could muster to reboard, but he did it. Sergeant Shields looked on shaking his head while Vin nestled himself back into his harness and blessed himself once securely locked in. Jock looked over to Sergeant Shields and shrugged his shoulders gesturing there was nothing he could do for the poor guy.

The final leg of the flight went without anybody getting airsick. It seemed like they all got their sea legs underneath them. The plane circled parts of San Diego and the Pacific Ocean as other planes landed. Some of the men caught a few glimpses of the surf breaking through the limited portholes in the fuselage while the plane was banking. Jock thought it was the neatest thing he had ever seen. The plane finally touched down at Camp Elliot at 1130 hours Pacific Time.

Disembarking from the plane, the first thing the Marines felt was the warmth of the sun and the clear, bright, beautiful sky. The next thing they noticed was the hustle and bustle of this huge base. One had to watch where they were going or you could be run over by another airplane, or Jeep, or Deuce-and-a-half. Everywhere you looked, the base was full of soldiers and supply trucks coming and going. Jock would be happy once they got off this airfield. It was making his head spin.

A caravan of military police in jeeps greeted the new Marines and herded them toward a seamlessly endless row of Quonset huts. They must have walked a mile before they were able to drop their gear within a compound segregated from the rest of the base. Sergeant Shields followed one of the MPs into the nearest building with a huge sign above the door bearing the words "Marine Combat Training Battalion."

Within ten minutes, Sergeant Shields came out of the building with two officers. Sergeant Shields issued a curt "Ten-Hut," and all four companies formed a semicircle and stood at attention to wait further instructions. The first officer walked down the four steps from the Headquarters porch and saluted the entire group. "Good morning, Marines," said the officer in a low baritone. "My name is Captain Faraday. I will be your CO for the remainder of your training. Lieutenant Blaine will be second in charge and will oversee the day-to-day operations with each of your sergeants. Your sergeant will remain as your NCO for this duration. You will be fed lunch at 1200 hours and at 1230 hours, you will board a convoy of Deuce-and-a-halfs just outside the mess hall. Your destination is Camp Pendleton where you will immediately begin amphibious tactics and maneuvers. Are there any questions?"

"Very well then. Lieutenant Blaine and Sergeant Shields, these MPs will escort you and your men to the mess hall. Once there, Instructors Sergeant Fitzpatrick and Culhane will link up with you.

They will assist you in preparing these Marines for their next assignment. Carry on." Sergeant Shields saluted the captain and ordered his Marines to double time it behind the MPs.

The company received (too much delight) fresh fruit and ham for lunch. They even had their choice of soda pop or iced tea. When the counter staff asked Jock what kind of pop he wanted, Jock just stood there dumbfounded. "Pop? What do you mean pop?" The cafeteria worker was getting a little annoyed with him. He figured he was from the New England area. It seemed like all those guys never heard of the word pop before. "Okay wise guy," cracked the man in the white apron and hat. "Do you want a pop or not?" Luckily, Vinnie was right behind Jock in line and interjected. "You mean soda pop. You know, like root beer or orange or Pepsi."

"That's right," exclaimed the miffed worker. "Why don't you just call it tonic like everybody else does!" queried Jock.

"Tonic! Tonic is for your hair grease ball!" The man behind the counter was getting really indignant now.

"Okay, okay, just give me a Coke," said Jock, trying to defuse the issue. But it was too late.

"Listen, chump, you've got three choices, root beer, iced tea, or a kick in the ass. Whadayawant?"

"I'll have a tonic," replied Jock, knowing full well this guy was going to come across the table any second.

"Get your skinny little ass outtahere before I—"

Vinnie stepped between Jock and the counter just in time. A second longer and the guy would have tried to reach over the counter to grab Jock by the collar. Vinnie knew the guy would have been sorry for trying such a move on Jock. The rest of the platoon behind Vinnie and Jock were getting a little aggravated with the delay. After the long flight, they were hungry and just wanted to eat. Vinnie gave Jock a nudge to move him forward to diffuse the situation.

When they finally sat down to eat, Vinnie gave Jock his Pepsi. "Here's your tonic," Vinnie said wryly. Jock just looked over at the guy behind the counter with daggers in his eyes. "Easy boy, just take it easy. You have got to control that temper of yours cuz someday I might not be there to cover your tail."

"I can't help it if the guy has a hair across his ass," quipped Jock in an elevated tone loud enough for just about everyone to hear.

Vinnie just stared down at his food shaking his head in disbelief.

"All right, Jock, you win. You just don't know when to shut it down do ya! I'm there for you, buddy, but you just have to ease up a bit, okay? Please, for me," resigned Vinnie. They ate their lunch in total silence.

After lunch, the platoon was herded over to an assembly area where they joined up with another platoon from the 1st Marine Division. They were given some time to write home but only to let their loved ones know that they arrived at their destination safely. By midafternoon, both platoons were transported to Camp Pendleton where they would commence amphibious assault tactics for the next ten days.

On the trip along Route 5 to Camp Pendleton, Jock and Vinnie got to talking with a few of the Marines from the 1st. Rumor had it that they were going to be shipped to Australia or New Zealand after their amphibious training here. One of the Marines from the 1st heard that the gals down under would do just about anything for a leatherneck. In fact, they were not shy at all. They would make the first move, the second move, and the final move. Jock and Vinnie were all smiles the rest of the way to the camp. The truth was it was nothing of the sort.

The vehicles arrived at the gate to Camp Pendleton by 1400 hours. Bus after bus with a few Deuce-and-a-halfs mixed in roared through the main gate kicking up a cloud of dust that could be seen clear across the base. The base itself was huge, comprising of over seven square miles of mountainous terrain to the west and isolated desert to the Southeast including 17 miles of Pacific shoreline.

Even before the convoy came to a complete halt at the receiving station, a squad of military police with batons in hand were poised to bark out orders. As each door and tailgate opened to let off the troops, the only sounds were of the MPs directing each load of men to fall in and form row after row of khaki-colored figures.

Once all the Marines were assembled, a towering behemoth of a man stepped out of a jeep to the left of the MPs. Jock guessed he must have been six foot six inches tall and weighed two hundred and seventy-five pounds of pure muscle. He walked from one end to the other end of every row inspecting every third or fourth man he came to. If he didn't like what he saw he would stop and express his dissatisfaction in one-way or another.

When he came to Jock, he stopped dead in his tracks and said, "Aren't you a little small to be a Marine?" Jock's response was colorful and to the point. "Sir, you know what they say, big guy, big balls, little guy, all balls." The man lowered himself a bit, looked directly into Jock's eyes and said "Hoo-rah Marine," and continued walking down the row. Jock felt a bead of sweat running down his cheek.

Finally, the big man came back to the front of the battalion. "My name is Lieutenant Colonel Anderson. I oversee the amphibious assault training program and will be responsible to teach you Marines the art of amphibious warfare. Our first exercise will start at 0430 hours tomorrow. Sergeant Culhane to my right and Sergeant Fitzpatrick to my left will escort you to the staging area where you will be broken up into platoons, issued combat and survival gear and instructed on what to do, how to do it, where to go, and when to execute. This will be drilled into you by some of our amphibious instructors. I cannot stress enough that the training for the next several days may save your life. Listen very carefully and do what Sergeant Culhane, Sergeant Fitzpatrick, and the instructors tell you. That is all, carry on."

At that point, Sergeants Culhane and Fitzpatrick introduced themselves to Sergeant Shields. Culhane spoke first. "Welcome to Camp Pendleton, Shields. If there is anything we can do to make your transition easier, just let Joe or me know. This set-up is a little different from usual. Both of us were stationed at Camp Elliot just north of here. Things were getting too tight to accommodate all the new recruits so they built this place in March of '42. Our old living quarters were tents. Now we got running water, a real floor under our feet, and windows. Can't beat that!"

"I appreciate your generosity, Bill, Joe. The same goes for me," replied Sergeant Shields. "If there is anything I can do to make your jobs easier, just let me know."

"Well, there is one thing," piped Sergeant Fitzpatrick. "You can make sure your boys don't get out of line with the female contingent on base. There's gotta be a couple of hundred dames here. Some are navy, others are Marine reservists working in administrative roles, and the rest are nurses. The last thing we need are a couple of horny Marines mucking up the works and cutting into our limited training time."

"You can count on it," responded Sergeant Shields curtly. "You have my word."

For the next few hours, the sergeants met with Captain Faraday and Lieutenant Blaine over at divisional planning to lay out the sequence of events to take place for that afternoon and tomorrow's first offshore amphibious maneuver.

Entering the large tent where the exercises were planned, Sergeant Shields could not help but be impressed with the professional execution of all the men and women applying their skills with the tasks at hand. There was no fraternizing, no squawking, and no recreational conversation going on. It was all business, serious business.

Captain Faraday had coffee and donuts brought in for this briefing. There were about thirty sergeants and instructors present. Most of them had been through this routine several times, but there were a few like Sergeant Shields that have never participated in amphibious doctrine. Actually, the entire doctrine was prepared just after Pearl Harbor. Mostly untried and unproven, but certain elements within the Marine Corps knew that the only way to beat the Japanese was to take one island after another the old fashion way... with blood and guts.

The plan was rather simple. Soften up the enemy by shelling the hell out of them day after day. Then send in frogmen the evening before the amphibious assault to assess the damage, survey any missed fortifications, and clear or at least identify any traps or mines that the assault troops may encounter. Then unleash a preemptive barrage of ordinance and lay down smokescreens with destroyers to mask the oncoming Marines in their Higgins Boats. The question was... would it work? So far, it had only been tried at Guadalcanal just a few months earlier with mixed results.

After the briefing, Lieutenant Blaine walked over to Sergeant Shields. "So, what do you think Sergeant?" asked the lieutenant. "Sir, I think a lot of these boys are not going to see their next birthday, but I also see that this is the only way to kick the enemy asses all the way back to their homeland."

"No one relishes placing our boys in harm's way, especially me," uttered Blaine. "Our job is to give them every advantage that we can, then pray to God that they succeed." Sergeant Shields nodded in the affirmative as Lieutenant Blaine walked away.

Sergeant Culhane and Fitzpatrick walked up behind Sergeant Shields and invited him over to their quarters for a cold beer. How could he refuse? It had been a week since he had a brew. This damn dry air around here was unbearable. Shields gladly accepted the invitation and the three of them walked back to their hooch discussing some of the finer points of the female persuasion. After a few beers and a shot of whiskey as a chaser they got to know each other well. Shields and Fitzpatrick did not meet eye to eye on many things, but there was a mutual respect among them. They would need it. When Shields finally left their hooch later that evening, he knew he would have to keep his eyes open and his head on a swivel to protect his men that he had become attached to. On reflection, he knew he was getting too close to some, and it troubled him. The walk back to his hooch cleared his mind.

Chapter VII

When the Going Gets Tough...

Sergeant Shields had his hands full. Still trying to acclimate himself to this new environment, the sergeant needed to gain control of his surroundings and lead his men through a new and different training protocol. One thing about the sergeant, he always made his men feel like they were the best of the best. So, his approach to this new training doctrine was not going to change much from his old tried and true methods. He knew he could count on his men the way his men could count on him.

After getting the lowdown from Sergeants Culhane and Fitzpatrick, Sergeant Shields was not surprised at their less than enthusiastic attitude towards the 3rd Battalion. It seemed almost as if they were just doing a nine-to-five job and then going home. Maybe they were just burned out from the frantic pace they've been put through since Pearl Harbor. Their cold and callous behavior was evident even to the swarm of newcomers. Sergeant Shields knew that he would have to be the one to lead by example, especially through the live fire exercises as they storm the beach in these new-fangled plywood boats called Higgins Boats. Sergeant Shields wondered to himself just what possessed the USMC to purchase landing craft made from plywood! Since when did plywood stop a bullet?

At 1500 hours the men were given a briefing on the new Higgins boat that they would be using to assault the fortified beaches the Japanese controlled. Lieutenant Blaine provided the men with the craft characteristics, its' capacity, and capabilities. Captain Faraday sat off to the right alongside Lieutenant Colonel Anderson and Second Lieutenant Bates observing the entire presentation.

Jock and Vinnie were seated in the front row of a hangar bay converted into a quasi-auditorium for occasions such as this. It could accommodate over 1000 people.

Lieutenant Blaine spoke in clear and concise diction. "Gentlemen," he started off. The one-third scale, mock- up craft behind me is called an LCVP, short for Landing Craft Vehicle Personnel. It is also known as the Higgins Boat, named after its inventor, Andrew Higgins. This craft is constructed mostly from mahogany, it has a displacement of 15,000 pounds, is thirty-six feet long, has a beam of ten feet, ten inches and a draft of three feet. It is powered by a Gray 225-HP diesel engine and can reach speeds up to twelve knots. It can hold 36 troops with gear and equipment or a jeep with twelve men. There are two .30-caliber machine guns mounted on the aft. This craft is going to take you from your troop transports and shuttle you onto the beaches occupied by the enemy. Are there any questions?"

Jock raised his hand immediately. Lieutenant Blaine gave him the "deer in the headlight" look and said, "Go ahead, Private." Jock felt a little uneasy and stuttered his first few words but was able to make himself clear.

"Just... err... what exactly prevents this boat from getting stuck on obstacles?"

"Good question," replied Lieutenant Blaine. "If you will notice, there is a head log, or a solid block of wood at the bow. This enables it to run full speed over obstacles, sandbars, and right up onto the beach without damaging the hull."

"How about protection?" asked Vinnie. "It sure doesn't seem like these boats are gonna stop machine gun fire!" Blaine paused for a second or two before he answered.

"You're right! There isn't much between you and the enemy. Steel is in short supply. The ramp is the only part of the boat that is made from steel. It does offer some protection. But, if the boat were made completely of steel, it would be much slower and less maneuverable, thereby giving the enemy a longer and better chance of zeroing in on the boats with artillery. Speed is essential for a successful beachhead."

Captain Faraday took over after that last response and discussed the methods of disembarking from the troop transports to the Higgins Boats. The Navy would soften up the enemy by maintaining a prolong and intensive barrage from their destroyers and cruisers.

While that is in effect, the troop transports will head towards the target objective and anchor approximately three miles out from landfall, just out of the reach of enemy guns. Or so they thought.

Once in position, netting will be dropped over the starboard and port side of the transports and the Higgins Boats will come along side. Each disembarking area will have its own identification such as Yellow-1 or Red- 4. The odd numbers will be on the port side and the even numbers will be on the starboard side.

The pilots of each Higgins Boat know their designated pick-up area. When the LCVPs are in place, you will be instructed by your squad leader to climb over the rail, down the netting and into the LCVPs. After your squad and supplies are secured, the pilot of each LCVP will proceed to its designated assembly area approximately 250 yards from the ship and will circle in a clockwise pattern if you are on the port side or a counterclockwise pattern if you are on the starboard side. This will continue until the entire first wave has assembled.

From that point, the LCVPs will be instructed to proceed to the rendezvous point, approximately two to three thousand yards from the beach. The LCVPs will form in a "V" pattern and remain in this line of departure until given the go-ahead to conduct offensive operations. The LCVPs will get you to within a few feet of actual dry land where the ramp will drop down and the wave commanders will signal you to storm the beach. The need for speed is essential.

The LCVPs will then return to the troop transports to pick up the second wave and conduct the exact same procedure. Captain Faraday illustrated this whole maneuver on the huge blackboard set up directly behind him.

Jock and Vinnie along with the rest of the company listened intently. You would have been able to hear a pin drop if it weren't for Faraday's recital. At the end of the lecture, Captain Faraday asked if there were any questions. No one said a word.

"All right Marines," quipped Faraday. "Tomorrow morning at 0430 hours you will report down to Pier 4, load onto the three troop transports and be given a free boat ride out in the Pacific Ocean." Each platoon will be given further instructions by their designated instructors the rest of the day. That is all and good hunting tomorrow."

As the 360 or so troops exited the converted hangar and reported back to their platoons, Vinnie and Jock caught up with Sergeant Shields. "Hey Sarge!" yelled Vinnie. "So whatdayathink?"

"I think tomorrow is going to be a devil of a day," replied Sergeant Shields.

"How do you mean?"

"I mean most of you guys have never been on a boat let alone know how to swim!! That's what I mean."

"Don't sweat it, Sarge," Jock said assuredly. "We can handle it. Right, Vinnie... Vinnie, right?"

"Oh... err... why do we need to know how to swim?"

"That's what I'm getting at," uttered the sergeant, slowly shaking his head left to right. With that, Vinnie and Jock just looked at each other and let Sergeant Shields walk away in his current state of mind.

After the final briefing by each squad leader back at the Quonset huts, the men were given a few hours of R and R. Jock and Vinnie made the most of it by playing cards with about half of their squad. Once they lost their fortune of about fifteen dollars each, they decided to take a stroll around the camp to see how the other half lived. They inadvertently ended up near the women's auxiliary at about 1700 hours. The shift change was taking place and both Jock and Vinnie got their eyes full of dame after dame coming and going through the commissary.

"Wow," whispered Vinnie, "it don't get any better than this."

"Yeah," gasped Jock. "I've never seen so many blonde dames in all my life!"

With their necks craned to watch skirt after skirt coming and going from the woman's auxiliary, Jock walked right into a group of three nurses bumping into a petite brunette and almost knocking her down. "Jeez, I'm sorry, are you all right? Did I hurt you? I'm so sorry." The brunette had dropped her side bag and began reaching for it, but Jock got to it first. "Please, let me get it," said Jock, still embarrassed about the whole ordeal. The other two nurses looked on and giggled.

"I'm okay," said the brunette. "Do you always walk without watching where you are going?"

"Only when I want to meet a nurse," replied Jock. "My name is Jock, Jock Donahoe. What's yours?"

"Monica."

"Well, Monica, it is a pleasure to meet you. This here is my buddy, Vin." But by now Vin was striking up his own conversation with the other two nurses.

"Well, you should be more careful where you're walking, Jock Donahoe," she replied. One of the other nurses interrupted their awkward moment and said they were running late for their training class.

"Hope we bump into you gals again," quipped Vinnie.

The girls started to walk away but Monica turned around and said, "It was nice meeting you, Jock Donahoe."

"Likewise," stuttered Jock, and before he could think of anything else to say, the nurses were turning the corner around a building.

"Nice going, you klutz," blurted Vinnie. "Next time leave the introductions to me."

"Pinch me," said Jock. "Make sure I haven't died and gone to heaven." Instead of pinching him, Vinnie wound up and gave him a shot in the arm.

"Could you feel that, buddy?"

Still smitten by the encounter, Jock's response was "Ahhh, did you say something?" They both grinned and started to walk back to their Quonset hut when Sergeant Culhane came around the corner and stepped right in front of them.

Jock almost walked right into the big man as the sergeant yelled out, "What the hell are you two doing over here!! I want your names and the company you're in."

Vinnie spoke first. "Sergeant Culhane, we were just—"

But before he could say another word, Culhane barked at them again. "The last thing I need is for you two morons to screw up my day! Now report back to your barracks on the double and do not ever let me catch either of you come anywhere near this part of the camp again. Do I make myself clear?"

"Yes, Sergeant Culhane," said Jock. "We just didn't know this area was off-limits." Culhane was in no mood to listen and just walked away.

"Whew," muttered Vinnie. "What an asshole. The guy needs to pull his shorts out from where the sun never shines."

"Cripes, Vinnie, let's just get back to the barracks. We don't need Shields breathing down our necks."

By the time Vinnie and Jock got back to their barracks, the whole platoon was watching a newsreel of the latest action in the South Pacific. The 1st Marine Division had taken Henderson Field, the prize of Guadalcanal. But the fighting was not over. The Japs were trying to take it back. Fierce sea battles were wagging as both sides tried to stop the supply of reinforcements. The Marine casualties were already around 1,500.

Japanese losses were estimated to be around 15,000, and the battle would likely go on for several more months. Many new lessons were being learned. Those lessons were costly, but they were going to be brought to bear starting tomorrow morning.

As the newsreel ended, most of the men hit their bunks to get as much sleep as possible before the training started. Vinnie and Jock were no exception.

At 0400 hours on the morning of December 21st, reveille sounded for the men of the 2nd Marine Division, 3rd Battalion, 6th Marine Regiment.

Within three minutes, they were assembled out in front of their Quonset huts. It was still pitch black when a series of pole mounted lights flicked on shining directly upon the rows of Marines. Most of them had to cover their eyes until they could get acclimated. An unfamiliar master sergeant was there to greet the still half-asleep troops. "Rise and shine gentlemen. Today is the first day of your amphibious assault training. You have twenty minutes to get breakfast and be back at this very spot to get transportation for your new and exciting adventure. That is all. Now get moving!"

The Marines had their usual allotment of powdered eggs, hash browns and coffee for breakfast. Then they had about five minutes to perform their daily rituals of hitting the crappers or whatever was necessary to get their sorry asses in gear. At 0430 hours, several Deuce-and-a-halfs were waiting with their motors running to swallow up 360 slightly jittery jarheads with their full gear for a short ride of a mile or so to Oceanside Beach Docks. This was where they would be making their amphibious assault debut. Jock and Vinnie were just about the last two to get on the last truck. This did not go unnoticed by Fitzpatrick and Shields.

The trucks pulled up to Pier 4 to disgorge the 3rd Battalion. The entire replacement battalion of inexperienced warriors were wondering just what the hell have they gotten themselves into. Roughly one-third of these guys had never been on a boat before. Now they were being herded like cattle onto troop transports, ferried to about three miles out to sea, and ordered to climbed down a net and off a perfectly sound platform into these bobbing and weaving plywood boxes called Higgins Boats in waters sixty feet deep.

Normally late-December weather would be sunny and around 70 degrees. Not today. There was a thick mist, and the temperature was hovering around 55 degrees. The 3rd Battalion had to wait on the dock until the 6th Replacement Battalion of the 1st Marine Division arrived. This gave the boys enough time to check their gear and light up a Lucky Strike or a Camel. Sergeant Shields came over to the platoon to try to ease some of the apprehension felt in the air. Shields immediately came right over to Jock and Vinnie and said "Donahoe, are you planning on walking up to the enemy saying you're sorry, let's be friends?" The squad let out a muffled laugh. It took Jock a few seconds before he realized Culhane must have seen the whole incident with the nurses yesterday and enlightened Shields with the details. "No Sarge, I plan on killing the enemy, then say who's next?" The rest of the platoon fell in with their own chatter. That's when the first elements of the 6th Replacement Battalion, 1st Marine Division arrived.

One by one, the men with about 60 pounds of gear in their backpack labored up the gangway and onto each troopship. Shield's platoon along with the rest of the 3rd Battalion boarded LST 74. LST stood for Landing Ship Transport. The 6th Battalion of the 1st Marine Division boarded LST 55 and the last LST received the mechanized equipment which consisted of some old and dilapidated "Pershing" tanks, some Deuce-and-a-halfs converted into Amtracs, and a variety of jeeps and howitzers.

At 0600 hours the three LSTs met up with a few vintage WWI destroyers, one cruiser that looked like it could barely stay afloat, and a couple of tugboats and tenders. This array of misfit ships represented the invasion force that was going to seize the mythical island of Ougatto occupied by three thousand soldiers of the Japanese Imperial Army. Their mission was to storm the beach and secure it until the mechanized equipment could be off-loaded. If this went as planned, they would do it again tomorrow. If it did not, they would do it again tonight.

Captain Faraday stood beside Lieutenant Colonel Anderson on the bridge of the cruiser hoping that the exercise goes flawlessly.

The cruiser represented the flag ship of the invasion force designated Task Force Jubilee. All communications and signals were to be initiated from this ship. Each troopship had lieutenants and/or second lieutenants that would receive the commands from the flag ship and disseminate the orders down the line to the sergeants and platoon leaders.

A lot of brass was watching from shore. Some new techniques were being used for the first time and a lot was riding on it. There were even spotter planes circling overhead with motion picture cameras recording every facet of the exercise. This was the first time that this method of observation and filming was being conducted. In the past, camera crews would be stationed on the ships and on shore.

At 0630 hours the flagship gave the signal to commence Operation Jubilee. The firing of smoke rounds from the destroyers and cruiser initiated the exercise. After about fifteen minutes of shelling, the LSTs maneuvered into their pre-established assembly areas and waited for their next set of instructions. Those came within five minutes and the word was given for all troops to climb down the cargo nets and into the Higgins Boats.

This phase took much longer than planned for. It seemed like the troops were climbing down in slow motion. The added 60 pounds of weight didn't help much. Some of the troops could not handle the extra gear without losing their balance trying to go over the side. A few of the men fell over either hitting water or the landing craft. It was an ugly sight. More time was lost because the unfortunate ones had to be pulled out of the water before they sunk to the bottom and others had to be treated for broken bones and the like.

It was becoming obvious that modifications were needed. From the shore, the brass could not see the mishaps in what seemed like a comedic display, but Captain Faraday and Lieutenant Blaine had front row seats. Captain Faraday put down his binoculars for a moment, stared into the vastness of the sea, and uttered to Lieutenant Blaine "This is a recipe for disaster. We must lighten their loads, or they will all drown before they get to shore." Lieutenant Blaine nodded and replied, "We could get their gear on the Higgins boats first and then let them climb down the cargo nets unimpeded?"

"Well, something has to be done and done fast," grimaced Faraday.

During the execution of getting into the Higgins boats, Jock finally made it down. Sergeant Shields and Vinnie were already in the boat extending a hand to Jock and others while others including the coxswain of each boat were busy pulling the unfortunate out of the water. It was miraculous no one drowned.

This phase of the operation was already twenty minutes behind schedule. That meant the Higgins boats had to make up time to the rendezvous area. This was easier said than done. The waves were kicking up. Some of the swells were six feet or more. Each Higgins boat operator had their hands full trying to keep the boats steady. It was literally an impossible task. Some of the Marines were throwing up making the conditions within the confines of the boat extremely slippery and dangerous. By the time all the LCVPs reached their rendezvous area, the schedule and men were in complete disarray. Nonetheless, the exercise continued.

The final signal was given, and the invasion force turned toward the shore in the open "V" formation. They were now about 2000 yards from the beach. The Wave Commanders gave the order to the coxswains for full throttle. This was it. Smoke screens were laid down and boat after boat made their mad dash to the shore. Within minutes the front ramps dropped down into the water and the Marines jumped into water three to four feet deep. Some of the men fell flat on their faces into the surf. Others were knocked over from the ensuing breaking waves behind them.

By 0730 hours the first wave of Marines landed, and the Higgins boats were headed back to the assembly area to pick up the next contingent. Captain Faraday and Lieutenant Blaine were still gritting their teeth from the earlier escapades.

By 0815 hours the second wave of reinforcements and some armored vehicles were arriving on the shores. Although not quite a complete success, Operation Jubilee did manage to proceed on its own accord. By 0900 hours, there were some 600 Marines with fighting vehicles entrenched on the beach with the first elements moving inland to gain a foothold in the underbrush. Jock, Vinnie, and Sergeant Shields were among the few that has moved inland. The rest of their platoon was just entering the tree line when smoke grenades went off all around them. It appeared the unseen imaginary enemy had laid a booby trap. The observers counted over half of Sergeant Shield's platoon dead.

Shields gathered up the remainder of his platoon and awaited further orders from his Second Lieutenant, Bernard Bates, III. He looked like he was about to pass out when he made it to the sergeant's position. Bernard was a graduate of Stanford and joined the ROTC in his sophomore year. He had no ambition to be in the service but was sort of coerced into it; given that his father was a retired admiral and saw action in the First World War. Father had insisted that his son learn the values of God, Country, Duty, or he would be cut out of any inheritance. So here he was, third in his class at Stanford, a member of every social club in the San Diego area, and now sharing a delightful rendezvous in the cold, wet morning with sand in every crevice of his body.

"Hey, Lieutenant," screamed Vinnie. "You don't look too good!"

"Can it, DiNapoli! Just give me the damn map so I can see where the hell we are!" Shields handed the map to the 2nd Lieutenant without saying a word. Bates fumbled about for his glasses for a minute or two before finding them in his shirt pocket, minus the left side of the frame. Vinnie and Jock could not help but grin seeing their CO completely flustered over the ordeal.

"Here, LT, let me show you where we are," said Sergeant Shields and began to point out the landmarks that he observed and the direction he thought they should be moving.

"Very well sergeant, I concur. Let's get the men rounded up to move out. Oh DiNapoli, you and Donahoe take point."

"Yes, sir," Vinnie called out with a trace of animosity in his tone.

It was just about 1000 hours when 1st platoon of I Company moved inland towards their objective; a makeshift landing strip that represented a Japanese air base vital to their supply route. A series of cardboard and wooden fortifications such as pillboxes and strongholds were set up along the route. Each one would have to be neutralized before any organized attack on the base could be orchestrated.

Second Lieutenant Bates called for his radioman. Private Harold

"Harry" Willis came running up almost tripping over a fallen log where Bates was standing. "Get with it Marine," yelled Bates. "If anything happens to that radio, I'll shoot you myself so help me God. Now get me Captain Faraday on the flagship pronto or I'll have your...!" But before Bates could finish his chastising of Willis, they simultaneously dove to ground only to look up to see it was the observation planes with cameras rolling. A loud chuckle came from the troops, but Sergeant Shields cut them off before it got out of hand. "Move it you sorry sons-of-bitches! We got an airbase to take!"

En route to meeting up with their remaining companies and elements of the 6th Battalion, no other surprises were encountered. Things were looking rather good. Both battalions hooked up as planned and scouts from both battalions were reporting in with enemy troop strengths and fortifications. The venerable Pershing tanks took care of the pillboxes, and flamethrowers were being used for the first time with incredible results.

The cardboard and wood pillbox mock-ups were incinerated in seconds. Now if only the real enemy pillboxes could be destroyed this easily thought Sergeant Shields to himself.

The enemy base consisted of an old overgrown grassy runway with a newly constructed tower and several wood mock-ups of barracks, hangars and miscellaneous buildings that gave the impression of a real live airfield. There were even several old 105-millimeter howitzers in sandbagged, embedded fortifications. The entire perimeter was surrounded with concertina wire and a few elevated outposts. In the middle of the runway sat cardboard mock-ups of Jap Zeros, Vals, and Nates. They actually looked real from where Jock was situated. Everyone waited in position for the signal to storm the base. One-half hour went by and still no word.

"What the cripes is going on?" quipped Vinnie. Within minutes, Sergeant Shields crawled up to Vinnie and Jock to give them and the rest of the squad the lowdown. "Seems like we have one of those so called SNAFUs. It appears that battalion did not bring enough smoke ordinance to carry out the mission. Until it arrives on the beach for the howitzers and mortars that are set up there, we wait."

"Hey, Sarge, who screwed up?" asked Jock.

Shields peered back to where the Second Lieutenant was positioned and said, "Guess who?"

"Well, at least this gives us some time to chow," responded Vinnie.

As if on cue, at exactly 1200 hours the smoke shells started falling on the airfield. Within fifteen minutes, the shelling stopped, and the word was given to take the field. Jock cut through the wire fence while crawling and his squad mates followed. Each man had smoke grenades that were to be used on every fortification, structure, and plane as they encircled the base culminating at the building with the large flag displaying the land of the rising sun. It was 1230 hours as the flag was taken down by troops of the 6th Battalion. The objective was achieved, but the time in which it took was dismal. They were supposed to have secured their objective by 1100 hours, one and a half-hour earlier.

Second Lieutenant Bates was on the radio with the flagship. He was informing his immediate superiors, Faraday and Blaine, that they had taken the enemy base and that most of his troops performed satisfactorily. This was not a unanimous assessment though. It appeared that the Brass were already briefed on the outcome of the exercise and were not entirely happy. Bates was the unfortunate recipient of this news. As soon as he got off the radio, he jumped all over the other NCOs.

"Your men made me look bad," he screamed. "All they had to do was go by the game plan and everything would have worked! But no, some of your Marines had to do things their way and muck up the works! I want to see Sergeant Shields and Sergeant Culhane over at my new command post in two minutes. The rest of you start returning to the beach for retrieval. Now move it!"

Shields and Fitzpatrick started to walk over to the new command post but got interrupted by Jock and Vinnie. "Hey, Sarge, what's up?"

"It seems like you two hotshots managed to get us in some shit with the Brass!" groused Fitzpatrick.

"Ease up Fitzpatrick," said Shields in a low tone. "We don't know who or what is the problem just yet. Let's find out before we jump to conclusions."

"Ease up! Like hell I will. These two clowns have been busting our balls since they arrived here." Sergeant Shields stood eyeball to eyeball with Fitzpatrick. "Listen up Fitzpatrick. Back off. If it is them, I will deal with it. Do I make myself understood?" Fitzpatrick was not going to be intimidated. "I understand one thing Shields. These two birds of yours better learn how to fly real soon." Fitzpatrick continued walking towards the command post. "Thanks for sticking up for us Sarge," said Jock. That guy has had it in for us the moment we stepped off that plane. All I can figure is that someone didn't like the way we climbed down the cargo nets or the way we scouted in the bush."

"You'll be the first to know once I get back. Now go head back with the rest of your platoon." Shields turned and walked off wondering just what Bates was going to deliver.

In the command post, Second Lieutenant Bates was sitting down eating a sandwich and drinking some tea. Sergeant Fitzpatrick was already talking with Bates when Shields walked in. "Sit down Sergeant Shields. Care for some tea?" asked Bates. "No sir, I'm fine thank you." Bates took a bite from his sandwich and swallowed. "As I was telling your associate here, it looks as if half of your platoon did not follow the proper procedures on this little exercise. As soon as a couple of your men had difficulty negotiating the cargo nets with their backpacks, almost all your other troops decided to take matters in their own hands and remove the backpacks and drop them down into the awaiting LCVPs. That is not standard doctrine. The Brass on the flagship noticed this little deviation and want to know who gave the order to change doctrine?" Second Lieutenant Bates continued drinking his tea. "No one did... sir," said Sergeant Shields. "This is what I call 'improvising.' It is something we instilled in the boys during boot camp."

"Well, it is something that you will 'un-instill' in them by tomorrow morning. Is that understood Sergeant Shields?"

"Sir, you saw what was happening to some of the Marines. We were lucky nobody got killed or even hurt. The backpacks are just too heavy for some to be climbing down from a rolling ship to a bobbing LCVP," pleaded Shields.

"I don't care," barked Bates. "The men are to become proficient at this procedure. This is why we have exercises... to train them, dammit!"

"With all due respect, sir, what good is the training if they all drown before they get into battle?" Bates stood up and stood face-to-face within one inch of Shields. There were a few seconds of dead silence before Bates responded. "Okay, Sergeant, what do you suggest?"

"I suggest, Lieutenant, that the packs be deployed before the men board onto the LCVPs so once the order is given, the men climb down with their bare essentials only: their rifle, ammo, and canteen. Each man would label their name onto the packs to make it quicker to identify once they board the LCVP."

There was another pause from the lieutenant. "I'll bring it up to the Brass at the evening briefing. Is there anything else you care to articulate, Sergeant?"

"No, sir," said Shields. "That's it." Second Lieutenant Bates sat back down to finish his sandwich and tea which had turned cold. Sergeant Fitzpatrick got up and walked over to the grub line with Shields. "I'll say one thing Shields, there ain't no flies on you." Shields grinned. "Well, let's see what happens tomorrow morning cause I could be in a pile of shit, then we'll see where the flies land."

At 0430 hours the next day, the men of the Second Division, Third Battalion were up and boarding their ground transportation back to the pier. "Another beautiful day in paradise," shouted someone in the back of the Deuce-and-a-half. The squad, still half-asleep, let out a few chuckles. Jock didn't think it was all that humorous.

"My idea of paradise is getting home after this war," said Jock. A few of the men seconded that remark.

On the ride over to the pier, the non-commissioned officers briefed each squad to the revised procedure for disembarking off the troop ship and onto the LCVP. The men were relieved that they did not have to lug their sixty-pound pack down the cargo nets.

"Finally, someone was using common sense," murmured Vinnie. A marker pen was handed out to each squad so that they could each write their name onto their pack. By the time the trucks arrived at the pier, all 360 packs were marked with the last names and first initial of each Marine.

This time the 6th battalion, 1st Marine Division was waiting for them. It seemed like things were getting to be a little more competitive.

By 0600 hours, both battalions and the mechanized components were loaded up and ready to steam. The temperature was climbing fast. It was already sixty-four degrees and the forecast called for sun and warm weather. This would make troop unloading a bit easier.

Sergeant Shields sat down with his company. The sun was just rising over his shoulder and Jock stared right at Shields as if he were a disciple from God. A disciple with a message that God was watching over them.

Shields started to speak breaking the trance Jock was in. "Gentlemen, as you know we are going to repeat the exact same maneuver today as we did yesterday. The only differences are you will not have to climb down the cargo net with your backpacks, and we are going to shave thirty minutes off our time today. Any questions?" Of course, Vinnie couldn't resist an opportunity like this and said "Sarge, I bet we can shave forty minutes off and beat the Sixth Battalion to the airstrip again!"

Some of the other Marines nearest to Vinnie nodded agreement. "DiNapoli, you gotta curb that enthusiasm of yours boy before it gets you into a world of hurt," responded Sergeant Shields. "I can't help it Sarge, I just want to kick somebody's ass." Just then, the orders were given to disembark.

The Marines plied their way through the gentle waves in the LCVPs. Smoke rounds were exploding about one thousand feet overhead giving the theater the more realistic scenario that the Marines were under attack from the enemy fortifications. In turn, the US Navy returned volley from their big guns with their own improvised smoke rounds. It looked like the real thing to anybody observing from a distance.

On board the flagship, Captain Faraday and Lieutenant Blaine conferred with some of the other officers regarding the change in doctrine. "I don't like it one bit," said Captain Faraday to a group of observers looking out over the port side toward the engagement area. "If these Marines can't handle a few extra pounds when they are not even under fire, what the hell are they going to do when the real shit hits the fan on the beach?" Just then a high-ranking officer and his entourage walked by and overheard the last remark made by Faraday. "Just a minute," quipped the unknown officer. Captain

Faraday and company turned to see who was eavesdropping, but then quickly stood at attention and saluted.

"I'll tell you what these Marines will do when the shit hits the fan, they will adapt, improvise, and overwhelm the enemy. Give these boys a chance, Captain. I think they will live up to our expectations."

As the officer and his subordinates walked away, one of the other officers asked in a muffled tone, "Who was that?"

The answer came back. "That was Lieutenant Colonel David M. Shoup." They all turned their attention back towards the beach and the unfolding amphibious assault exercise.

The ramp dropped down to unload its live cargo. Jock and Vinnie along with Sergeant Shields were the first ones into the water. Sergeant Shields waves the remaining platoon to follow. All around them, Higgins Boats were disgorging their contents onto the beach. Jock was getting an adrenaline rush just seeing hundreds and hundreds of Marines charging for the shoreline. He thought to himself that this would be what it is like during a real assault, only bullets would be flying and men dropping into the blood red surf. Jock shook himself out of those thoughts and continued to make for the beach as hard and fast as his legs would take him through the waste deep water while fighting the outgoing tide.

As soon as the first elements reached the beach, they scurried up to and dropped behind a slight berm about 25 yards in from the water's edge. From there the recon squads scouted the tree line in the hopes of identifying enemy emplacements. Some new fortifications were found. Basically, just some sandbagged entrenchments with mock machine guns sticking out over the bags. As soon as those emplacements were dealt with by the Pershings, it was determined to be clear, and the rifle squads, mortar squads, and B.A.R. teams would then zig zag across the remaining open beach until reaching some of the low-lying underbrush at the edge of the canopy providing protection. Once the platoon was in a secure position, Sergeant Shields motioned the radioman Willis over to his side. This time he didn't stumble. Shields then signaled for the position and status of the other platoons and to await further orders. Then, the second phase of the operation could commence with the delivery of the remaining mechanized platoons.

Within one hour of establishing the beachhead and that sufficient supplies were being off-loaded and secured, the Marines were ready to thrust forward into the woods. The conditions were wet from the heavy rains the previous evening making the advance tepid at best. The Marines slogged along toward the enemy base while watching for booby- trap mock-ups and other devices designed to slow or stop the seven hundred or so Marines from advancing.

Just as the first wave of Marines entered the tree line, a mighty roar of seven Convairs buzzed overhead with fictional markings on each tail. There was much consternation about changing the US Army markings on the plane to anything other than Army for fear that someone not involved with this huge exercise would send out an alert or worse, shoot at the squadron. So, the Brass made sure all branches of the military received ample notice.

Each plane dropped what appeared to be a bomb from its fuselage. Only these bombs were made from papier-mâché and broke apart upon impacting the ground. In some cases, the fake bombs would just burst apart under the plane's fuselage before the pilot got a chance to drop it on its intended target.

With observers mixed in with each platoon, they estimated the casualty rate and informed each platoon leader which of their guys were now dead. At the end of the first assault, the tally was seventy-two Marines dead; another forty-seven wounded, meaning a total of a hundred and nineteen were picked out by the observers and informed they could not proceed with the mission. The amphibious assault squadron was now down to five hundred and eighty men.

"We were lucky they didn't come in while we were still all on the beach," said Sergeant Shields to Second Lieutenant Bates. Bates was still emptying water out of his boots and cared less about the phantom casualties. His main objective was to impress the brass by reducing the time to overtake the base. "Let's get moving sergeant; we've got a job to do. There will be no more dilly-dallying around. I want that base in our control before the 1st battalion knows we are even in the neighborhood!"

"Yes sir," said Shields. "Second platoon move out. Third platoon take the left flank. Fourth platoon take the right flank. First platoon take the rear." Jock and Vinnie were in the 1st platoon.

Treading deeper into the woods, the Marines encountered new obstacles that were not there during the first exercise. Trip wires were strewn all about. At each end of a tripwire, cans half-filled with pebbles were attached. As soon as a leatherneck hit the wire, the can would shake making enough racket for the observers to take notice and start counting new casualties. Sergeant Shields was now getting peeved at the second lieutenant's careless attitude.

"LT," whispered the sergeant, "we are getting clobbered by these booby traps. Can we slow it down a notch before we end up walking into the base with no troops at all?"

"How many have we lost?" Bates asked. "We're down to 60 percent strength, sir."

"All right then, pass the word, the next man that sets off one of those contraptions has to swim back to the troopship... with full gear on his back."

This was not making Shields a happy man, especially when Bates then asked for the position of the 6th Battalion, 1st Marines. Word had it that the 6th Battalion had taken exceptionally light casualties and were within striking distance to the enemy base.

Bates was indignant about that. They were making great time but somehow the 6th Battalion was ahead of them. To make matters worse, Bates ordered the entire company to double-time it straight to the airstrip regardless of obstacles.

2nd Platoon was down to 45 percent strength by the time they were on the outskirts of the airstrip. The other platoons were at similar numbers.

Situated on a knoll but considered too low to be called a hill, Bates and Shields could observe portions of the 6th Battalion already surrounding the rear of the enemy base. The 6th was just waiting for Second Lieutenant Bates to inform them that they were now in position. Bates had a hard time controlling his emotions, so he ordered Sergeant Shields to contact the 6th Battalion and inform them that there appeared to be a large enemy force gathering on their right flank apparently ready to ambush them as soon as the 6th makes its final assault. Of course, none of this was true but Bates was standing over the sergeant listening to every word, making sure he did not deviate from his orders. The fact was the enemy had dug in with a couple of mock machine gun nests and mortars exactly where Shields had described, but nobody knew. This ploy would make the 6th pause and reassess the situation before exposing their forces to an unknown adversary.

Within two minutes, the fireworks began. Only the fireworks did not belong to the attacking forces. From out of every crevice and hole, and from behind every fallen log came enemy mortar squads lobbing smoke shell after smoke shell along the perimeter of the base. In the mayhem, Jock and Vinnie along with the rest of the 1st platoon were able to sneak up on a couple of the unsuspecting mortar squads and silence their initiative. Their action was the only thing that saved the other platoons from complete annihilation. The 6th Battalion had suffered the same consequences as the 3rd Battalion only they did not have a platoon watching their six.

After the smoke cleared it was evident that both battalions were Almost decimated, but they were able to reach and control their objective. Both Battalion Commanders stood in the middle of the airstrip with grim looks on their faces. They knew what would be coming when the observers report to their superiors with the results.

On their way back to the troop carriers, Second Lieutenant Bates called for Jock, Vinnie, and Sergeant Shields. When they arrived, Bates extended his hand to each of them. "If it weren't for your sergeant here to keep a platoon in reserve and if it wasn't for your initiative to subdue the mortar squads, we probably would have been wiped out and I would be eating crow for dinner tonight. I just want to say job well done."

Still fuming over Bates's tactics to deceive his brothers at arms, Sergeant Shields took the opportunity to display his pride and his admiration to Jock and Vinnie and to the rest of the platoon. "These are the type of guys that are going to kick the Japs' asses clear across the Pacific. You can count on it," beamed the sergeant.

The 1st platoon was feeling rather good about themselves that evening. Cases of warm two-point-two beer were brought in for all the Battalions. This would be the last time they would be consuming any alcoholic beverage of any kind for a while. Word had it that they would be shipping out soon.

The next morning, Jock woke up with a dull ache in his head. He could not understand how a couple of beers could do this to him.

Cripes, Jock handled a lot more beer than this before without any hangover. So, he popped a few aspirin from his supply locker and looked at his watch. It was only 0330 hours and everyone in the barracks laid in a comatose state.

He tried to get back to sleep but couldn't. The dull ache in the back of his head refused to relent. Jock lay motionless in his bunk thinking of Jeanne. He missed her more than he realized possible. He could almost feel her, almost smell her. A warm smile developed on his face. Then the sound of a bottle cap being pried off got his attention. It was Vinnie, swigging down a warm brew. He must have stashed it in his fatigues when they were leaving the PX for the night. "Hey, what the hell are you doing?" whispered Jock. "I'm having a nightcap mate, you want some?"

"No, I don't need any more of that skunk piss," retorted Jock. "Suit yourself," as he chugged the remaining warm liquid down his throat. About ten seconds later, Vinnie let out a loud burp waking half the squad. Jock just buried his head under the blanket and willed himself back to sleep.

Just before dawn, the whole barracks shook making the disheveled leathernecks jump up from their bunks. Most of the guys in the lower bunks could not avoid hitting their heads on the bottom of the steel framed upper bunks. "What the hell is going on?" screeched about half of the platoon as another tremble got the attention of the true die-hard sleepers.

Sergeant Shields came storming into the barracks yelling at the top of his lungs for his men to grab their socks and hold on to their cocks and make a beeline to the air raid shelters.

"What's going on Sarge?" asked Jock.

"Fugos," responded the sergeant.

"What the heck is a Fugo?" asked Vinnie. Shields quickly gave the huddled group a heads-up on what was occurring.

"It appears that some coast watchers reported high altitude balloons off the coast. They call them Fugos. I don't know why in hell they call them that... they just do. Then base sentries sounded the alarm when some balloons were sited heading directly for Camp Pendleton. What you just heard was a squadron of Marine flyboys in their P40s racing balls to the wall to intercept."

"All of this for some misdirected hot air balloons?" asked Vinnie with a confounded look on his face. "Let's just get to the damn shelters and I'll fill you in once we get there!" hollered Shields as he led his men to the bomb shelters.

Once inside the shelter, Sergeant Shields gave the whole platoon the skinny on what was happening. "Okay, the latest Intel has revealed that the Empire of the Rising Sun has been working on incendiary devices. That's firebombs to those of you that never got past the third grade! These incendiary devices are strapped to hydrogen filled balloons, which originate from Japan and get caught up in the jet stream and eventually reach our country via the Pacific Ocean. A timer set to a fuse is devised to go off based on some Jap scientist's calculations as to when it reaches our shores. Once the fuse is set off, it ignites the incendiary device, burns the straw and paper and the balloon crashes to the ground and starts forest fires or any fire where combustibles are present... that's anything that burns for you idiots again. To date, there have only been rumors with a few civilian observations reported up in Oregon and Washington... until now." The platoon sat in the dimly lit shelter still trying to comprehend the events unfolding.

The entire base was in a state of confusion and turmoil. Many Marines were still scurrying about and some of them stopped to look up at the few balloons that did make it over the camp. Those that spotted the balloons were more amused and decided there was no threat, so they started to go back to their barracks where they left their warm bunks and warmer dreams only to be greeted by some mean looking MPs with their rifles slung at the ready. They meant business.

The order was given to let the three or four balloons continue and pass over the base until out of the populated area. At that point, the flyboys were instructed to shoot down every last one of them.

Within the hour the excitement had waned. The Marines' first order of business once they left the safety of the shelters was to reconnoiter the areas that the pilots shot down the balloons. If any were found, they were not to approach them but to cordon off the area and report their findings to their superiors. From there, specialized bomb technicians would ascertain if the device posed any threat. This would take the remainder of the day.

Four thousand military personnel participated in the exercise.

Of the six balloons shot down, all were found to be capable of inflicting serious damage had it not been for the timers malfunctioning. The causes of the malfunctioned timers were determined to be from the altitude and exposure of severe weather conditions crossing the Pacific Ocean.

Later that evening, the entire base personnel was briefed on the devices. "Very clever those Jap bastards," quipped Vinnie. "Yeah, we could have burned to death in our sleep," rebuffed an unknown Marine. "All the more reason we got to finish these nips off once and for all," as Jock looked at some of the debris of a balloon minus the incendiary device.

The Marines were instructed not to mention this event in any letter to home. The last thing the US Government wanted was a panic on their hands with the civilian population. It would be difficult enough just to deal with the politicians on this one.

Sergeant Shields carefully folded up the remnants of a balloon he found, and started back to the hanger where the debris was being stored for further evaluation when Vinnie called out "Hey Sarge, why not keep it as a souvenir?" Sergeant Shields stopped just as he was halfway out the door, turned around and walked deliberately over to DiNapoli. Vinnie could feel the short hairs on the back of his neck rise. "There will be plenty of souvenirs to claim when we kill every last Jap that is trying to kill us." Shields turned back to the direction he was headed and proceeded to his intended destination. Not another word was spoken from the platoon as he disappeared around the corner. The men were quiet for another reason.

Sam and Chaz had just heard that they were getting their deployment orders tomorrow. This made Jock and all the men in the barracks anxious and a bit excited on what laid ahead.

Chapter VIII

Honed to a Sharp Edge

Early on the morning of December 24, 1942, Jock's battalion, now designated as a Replacement Battalion, along with the rest of the 6th Regiment received word that they would be shipping out very soon. Scuttlebutt had it that they would make one stop at some remote island in the Central-Pacific. No one knew where for sure. Some guessed it might be Samoa. A brigade of Marines defended this small chain of islands as there was strategic value for ships to refuel and resupply before moving to their destination.

In Jock's case, the vessels carrying the 6th and 8th Regiments would disembark upon arrival. The remaining vessels in the task force would link up with other vessels from various ports of the world forming a massive armada before steaming to their pre-determined destination. Upon arrival of the 3/6 and the 2/8, they would continue with some limited amphibious training and jungle tactics. In a few days, their voyage would be the first of its type for many a Marine. Most would get acclimated to the pitching and rolling of the open seas, but some would never get used to it. It was going to be a very long journey via a circuitous route.

In the letters he was writing to home, Jock was careful not to divulge where his battalion was heading and when. All they could say was that they were shipping out to destinations unknown. Nobody wanted to be the one that would jeopardize the lives of their fellow Marines. The standard jargon was "loose lips sink ships."

One of Jock's letters to father went like this:

Dear Dad,
Hope this letter finds you well. I am just finishing up amphibious training here. It was tough and I got seasick a couple of times, but then again so did just about everyone else. My buddy Vinnie and I are still together. We make the best poker partners on the base. I'm up almost two hundred bucks. You'll find half of it with this letter, I hope. No need for me to be carrying so much money. It only weighs me down. The chow is pretty

good here and I have started to gain the weight back that I lost at Parris Island. All in all, things are pretty swell. We can't wait till we can kick some Jap ass. How are sis and brother doing? Some of the guys still want me to arrange a date for them with Evelyn. Maybe I should start a lottery or something and split the proceeds with sis. The west coast is beautiful, but it sure doesn't beat back home. I'll take the Charles River any day. Well, I need to make this letter short because the lights go out in two minutes. Don't worry about me. Give my best to everybody.
Jock

His letter to Jeanne would have to wait. The men in his barracks were packing their gear and squaring away for their next adventure. His mind was racing fast forward trying to visualize his actions when encountering the enemy. Would he be brave under fire or turn and run the second he sees a dead, bloody Marine? Jock was determined to prove his mettle under fire. "Donahoe!! Snap out of it," roared Sergeant Shields, walking into the barracks. It was 0800 hours, and the Marines were supposed to assemble outside at 0755. Jock jumped to his feet and stood at attention. The barracks were empty except for the two of them. All the other Marines had already completed their perfunctory duty and were at attention out in the yard except for Jock.

Shields walked up to Jock and came within one inch of his face. "Donahoe, what is the problem? Never mind, I don't want to know. You got thirty seconds to get your skinny ass in line with the other Marines or I am going to kick that skinny ass so hard you will not be able to sit down for a week. Is that understood Marine?" By this time Jock's heart was pounding through his chest and sweat was beading down his face. "Sergeant, yes sergeant." Jock was outside in formation within twenty seconds.

The battalion was standing at attention when two jeeps pulled up. The first jeep had three MPs in it, and they all jumped out as soon as it came to a stop directly in front of the battalion. The second jeep had a driver, one MP, and an officer.

Second Lieutenant Bates shouted out, "Ten-Hut" and the entire battalion come to correct military stance. The officer stepped out of the jeep and positioned himself directly in front of the Marines. "At ease Marines. I make it a point whenever I can to meet the men who are willing to sacrifice their lives for their country. Let me make something perfectly clear. I don't want you to die for your country. I want you to have the enemy die for theirs!" There was a controlled "Hoo-rah"(1) from the men. The officer motioned Bates and the NCOs to form up near his jeep. "I have heard good things about your men" the officer murmured. "Godspeed and clear skies on your voyage." The officer jumped back into his jeep and sped off with his detail.

Sergeant Shields had the men dismissed except for Jock. "Donahoe, let's take a little stroll." About 100 feet into the walk, Shields comes to a stop and asks Jock what is going on.

"Sarge, I just got to thinking how I would react once the bullets start flying and Marines start falling. I got scared thinking that I would not live up to your expectations and keep the trust of my fellow Marines." They found a bench just a few feet away and sat down with Jock waiting for Shields to respond.

"Every Marine thinks the same thing at one time in their lives. There is really no way anyone knows that answer until that time comes. You are not alone, son. One thing I can say for certain. I am not worried about you; I worry about the Marines I don't know. Now get back to your squad. We have a busy day today."

Later that morning, scuttlebutt in the barracks had it that they were to be a replacement battalion for the leathernecks on Guadalcanal. No one knew for sure, but the 1st Marine Division casualty rate had climbed much faster than anticipated. This was not only primarily due to combat but to malaria and other island- bred maladies. There was a shortage of penicillin and most of the hospital ships were filled to capacity with various combat related wounds, dysentery, malaria, heat exhaustion and of course, fallen soldiers.

"Great, "just great" said one of the Marines. "The 1st Marine Division gets all the glory, and we have to go in and clean up their stinking mess. Ain't there no justice in this world?" Jock and Vinnie just glared at the unknown Marine. "I heard that they received 30 percent casualties storming the beaches. I wouldn't call that glory," quipped Jock.

Now Vinnie had to get into the act. "Yeah, they are our fellow Marines that died on that island. I don't mind too much if we can unload right onto a beach without getting shot at."

The unknown Marine wouldn't let it go. "Where's the fun in that?"

"You got a warped sense of principles," quipped Jock to the Marine.

After an early lunch (about 1100 hours), the battalion was given orders to rendezvous at the parade grounds. From there, they were to be loaded up into Deuce-and-a-halfs for a ride up to Camp Elliot, the former USMC Training Depot before Pendleton in San Diego became the new official post. Nobody knew why they were going up. They just knew that they were being shepherded up there as quickly as possible and to wait for further orders. Same old story for the Marines, hurry up and wait.

The vehicles came to life and the first couple of Jeeps loaded with MPs led the way, followed by the battalion commander's entourage, and then the Deuce-and-a-halfs filled with leathernecks. Taking up the rear was another couple of jeeps loaded down with MPs.

It was a dusty ride up to Camp Elliot. The ground was powder-keg dry from lack of rain and each vehicle kicked up its own cloud of dust. Many of the Marines tied handkerchiefs around their faces to keep from breathing in all the dust and engine fumes. They also kept their eyes closed. It was 1200 hours when the convoy finally made it to a paved road called Highway 1. The vehicles picked up speed. The guys in the tail end of the Deuce-and-a-halfs were actually the luckiest of the group. They were able to peer out from the canvas flap and gaze out along the curved roads to see the deep blue Pacific Ocean and the waves breaking against the jagged rocks sticking out of the water. It was a sight many of the leathernecks would not soon forget.

"Take a look at this, will ya?" squawked Vinnie. "I have never seen waves this big in all my life." Jock had to switch seats with Vinnie to look out.

As Jock strained his neck to get a full view, he felt two hands on his back and then a powerful shove. Jock felt for sure he was going to end up as roadkill, but the same two hands that would have ruined his day were the same two hands that grabbed the back of his belt and pulled him back in. The other guys in the truck let out a huge laugh on Jock's behalf. He was still as white as a ghost and a little shaky when the laughter subsided.

"Sorry, buddy, I had to do it. It was just too damn easy. I'm real sorry, Jocko. I'll make it up to ya," said Vinnie very seriously.

"That's okay," said Jock. "You may just want to sleep with your eyes open for the rest of your life." The truckload of Marines chuckled again.

The convoy carrying the battalion arrived at the gates of Camp Elliot just after 1245 hours. Over to the west of the main gate was a rail yard bristling with tanks and armored vehicles strapped down to the flatbed railcars. There must have been a hundred railcars because you could not see the end of it. "Shermans," yelled out one of the Marines in the back of the truck with Jock and Vinnie. "Would ya look at them babies!"

"Those things are gonna tear up everything they go up against."

"How do you know so much about them?" quizzed Vinnie to the Marine. "Cuz, I read about 'em in Popular Science. Their actual name is the M4A3, and they will do 'bout 30 miles per hour and shoot a 5-inch projectile almost two miles. The nips have got nuthin' like 'em. Just wait and see," replied the Marine. "Death trap seems to be the more likely word for them," replied Jock. "You're a sitting duck in one of those things. I'd rather be behind one than inside of one." Vinnie and some of the other guys nodded their heads in the affirmative.

Upon a closer look on board each railcar revealed a various assortment of scout cars, Willys Jeeps, Half Tracks and LVTs. The Marine that apparently knew so much about the Shermans was almost as giddy as a little boy at Christmas time admiring all the other new toys of destruction sitting on the railcars just waiting to be pressed into duty.

As the last vehicle passed through the main gate the entire convoy grinded to an abrupt halt. "Welcome back to Camp Elliot, boys," rumbled a very serious-looking MP as he rounded the corner to the back of the truck. Jock noticed several other MPs performing the same perfunctory duty to the remaining trucks in the convoy.

By 1300 hours the entire battalion along with a few other companies from parts unknown were led to the camp's canteen where they were given coffee and cornbread. At 1330 hours a high-level officer and his entourage entered the canteen and immediately drew everybody's attention. From where Jock and Vinnie were sitting, they could not see just how important their visitor was, but it didn't matter. The nearly one-thousand Marines stood up at attention and saluted. They remained at attention for several minutes until a voice emanating from a microphone told them "at ease and sit down."

The tall man with glasses paused and looked directly into the crowd of Marines for what seemed like an eternity. Then he spoke. "Marines... just that one word, Marines, makes our enemies piss their pants." The audience let out a loud cheer. Then the officer spoke again. "Let's not think for one moment though that they will not kill you as they are soiling their own fatigues. They have been trained to kill as many of us as they can until being killed themselves. You would not be here if you couldn't cut it in Boot Camp. Your hard work, discipline, and unwavering patriotism prove to me there is no enemy on earth that can beat a United States Marine."

"Soon, you will be sent into harm's way. Some of you may not come back. Many of you will see a comrade fall. That is why you are here today, to hone your skills to a razor's edge. After this exercise, you will be sent back to Pendleton until the 30th of the month, shipped to a classified location in the Pacific to merge with elements of the 2nd Marine Division, 2nd, and 6th Regiments, as Replacement Battalions. From there, you will receive additional training until deployed to wherever Uncle Sam beckons you. Godspeed and God bless all of you." The steely-eyed officer left the wood podium as the entire audience stood back up at attention. "Does anybody know who the hell that guy is?" asked some Marine sitting just behind Jock and Vinnie. "Yeah, shit for brains" growled an MP in the aisle. "That was the Commander of the Marine Corps."

The exercise started immediately after the speech and would continue late into the night. The plan laid out was getting to be monotonous to Jock and Vinnie, always going over and over the same beach landing and setting up a flanking probe to determine the enemy's strengths or weak points. They were waterlogged from jumping into the four-foot-deep surf time after time. Their skin was chaffed from slogging through the surf and onto the beach, falling into a prone position and crawling up through the sand only to get up again and hightail into the tree line. From there, they would improvise a defensive perimeter until all assets were ready to push forward. Vinnie couldn't wait to have one day of being totally wet-free. Perhaps then his inner thighs would start to heal, or at least stop bleeding. Jock was no worse for wear. He had developed an ear infection. Sometimes he couldn't maintain his balance and fell frequently into the water saturating all his gear. These had to be the worst days of their training.

When all was done, the new battalions were battle-ready. Seven hundred and twenty Marine replacements were eager to take on the Japanese Imperial Marines anywhere, anytime.

The trip back to Camp Pendleton late in the evening was quiet. No one had anything to say. Perhaps they were just too tired or perhaps they were thinking about the next time they were to land on a beach. Some far away island nobody ever heard the name of, full of Japs just waiting to cut them down as they lowered the ramps on their Higgins boats. In any event, it didn't seem to bother Jock after the words spoken to him by Shields. He had not heard a peep from Vinnie in over an hour. "Silence is bliss," he thought to himself.

Extending for over a mile in length, the convoy got back to camp just after midnight. Both battalions were greeted with their mail already placed on their bunks. Most of the Marines just plunked down on their bunks once they stripped their wet, grungy clothing off. The guys didn't even think that it was actually Christmas. They were just too damn tired to care. The good news was they have the next twenty-four hours off and there were activities planned later in the day. One of those activities was supposed to be a Christmas show. It was rumored that a celebrity would be on the base, but nobody knew whom. They would have to wait and see. The snoring from the barracks full of Marines did not stop Jock and Vinnie from reading their letters from home.

Vinnie found out his older sister had twins and they named the boy Vinnie, after him. Vinnie let out a muffled holler trying to keep his excitement in check, but it didn't work as he woke some of the Marines nearest to him that were starting to doze off. He didn't care about that. He was going to have a nephew to spoil when he got home after the war. Maybe he would bring home some souvenirs from across the Pacific. Jock got two letters, one from Jeanne and the other from his buddy, Eddy McAfee. He opened the letter from

Jeanne first.

Dear Jock,

Hope all is well with you. We all miss you very, very much. I am still working at the laundry on Saturdays. Mr. Hurley sends his regards. College is very hard. I'm having difficulty with biochemistry, but I think I'll get through it. I didn't think Saint Elizabeth's would be so hard. Well, one semester done and only two more years to go! It seems like eternity. Just like you not being here. Time goes by so slowly. I have some upsetting news for you. My father is sick. The doctors say he has cancer of the esophagus. He refuses to believe them and continues to smoke. He coughs all day and all night long. I feel awful for having to tell you this for I know you have plenty of other things to worry about, but I thought you should know. He asks for you all the time. So does mother. Your dad came into the laundry a couple of Saturdays ago. He looks fine. He is such a handsome man. Now I know where you get your looks from. Oh, I almost forgot to tell you that the police caught a gang of hoodlums trying to burn down Brighton High School. It appears that they were not too effective or for that matter very bright. They had just filled some cans with gasoline and were pouring the gas around the outside of the school when one of them was still smoking a cigarette and the sparks ignited the can he was pouring. He suffered terrible burns. Some of the others got burned too trying to help him. The only damage done to the school was to the bushes. It turned out that none of them attended Brighton High. They were from Hyde Park. The rumor is that one of them was dumped by a girl whose father happens to be the principle, Mr. O'Leary. Now that is taking things a little too seriously don't you think? My dad says they ought to put them in the brig and throw away the key or give them to a couple of US Marines for a few hours. That would straighten them out. Well, time to say so long for now. Please watch yourself and finish this war as soon as possible. We have some catching up to do if you know what I mean.

Your girl always.
Jeanne

Jock was getting a little homesick now. He missed all the little things like teasing Jeanne's kid sister and just hanging around down at the Egyptian with his buddies. Those days were gone now and probably gone forever. He knew things changed, but he didn't have to like it. Jock carefully refolded his letter from Jeanne and placed it with his other stash of personal items. Then he opened the next letter.

Hey, Jocko. How are things? My parents wrote me that you got into the Marine Corp. That's swell. I always knew you would find a way. It took a while, but I was able to track you down with some assistance from a new friend of mine. She works in the Naval Personnel Department at Pearl. I met her and a group of her friends at a club when some buddies and me got some leave in Honolulu. I can't tell you her name. I don't want anybody to know so that she doesn't get into trouble with her superiors. But anyways, if it weren't for her, I would have never been able to track you down. In case you didn't know, I was in the thick of things on Guadalcanal and came out without a scratch. I don't mind telling you I was scared shitless, but then so was everyone else. The Japs had every square inch of the beach mapped for cross firing. We lost a lot of good guys. One of the guys no more than two feet from me as we were storming the beach disappeared in the blink of an eye. Nobody ever found out what happened to him. Best guess is he got struck by an anti-aircraft round that just obliviated him. I've been told the Japs will use any weapon at their disposal. Poor soul, he was a good kid.

I think the worst part was at night. We'd be sitting in our foxholes and then hear a scream, then some shooting. I found out that those bastards would sneak out of the jungle at night and bayonet our guys in their foxholes. I'll tell you I don't think I'll ever close my eyes again during the night. The good news is our battalion is scheduled to go back to Australia for some R and R. Word is that we will be stationed there for at least a couple of months licking our wounds, getting replacements for the guys we lost. That means we are gonna have to baby-sit the newbies for a while. Who knows, perhaps we will be running into each other sometime soon. Well. I gotta keep this short, for the war effort and all. Remember, loose lips sink ships. Keep safe my friend.

Semper Fi,
Eddy

Jock read Eddy's letter over again. It was good to hear from him. Jock kept on wondering if maybe they would find each other halfway around the world. Ten minutes later, Jock joined the rest of the Marines in a rhythmic drone of snoring.

No reveille, no shouting, no banging of batons against the bunks. Jock thinks to himself how he could get use to this. Some of the other Marines were up, tidying up the mess each left at the foot of their bunks. On any other day, a Marine would be punished by running 5 miles in full gear and then getting latrine duty. Not this day. It was Christmas. Better yet, it was 0730 hours, and all was still quiet.

Later that morning, prayer was offered to all those that wanted. The troops were herded into groups of that religious persuasion and then directed to tents that serve as makeshift churches, synagogues, or whatever each Marine's choice of worship was. There were just too many Catholics to accommodate in the tents that were set up, so Mass was conducted under the open skies of sunny Southern California. Jock and Vin received the host at Communion. Jock didn't realize Vin was a devout Catholic also.

After the religious ceremonies were over, everyone got served turkey, stuffing, potatoes, squash, green beans, and gravy. There was also the canned cranberry sauce to go around. There were even bottles of wine distributed out among the rank and file. Naturally, that seemed to disappear first. Father Joseph McCormick walked over to where Vin and Jock were sitting. He noticed the cross around Jock's neck.

"That is a magnificent cross," said the priest with a notable Boston Irish accent.

"Thanks," said Jock. "It was given to me by a friend of the family back home."

"And where might that be?" asked the father.

"Brighton, Brighton Massachusetts."

"Well Saints Alive, a fellow Bostonian! I'm from West Roxbury, Holy Ghost Parish." The two of them shared a few cordial moments then Father Joe said his goodbyes and performed a ceremonial blessing to Jock and the group of guys surrounding him.

"May God be with you Father," Vin blurted out as Father Joe walked away and over to the next bunch of Marines.

After their feast, Jock and the rest of the squad had their chance to play volleyball against another rival squad from Company B. Volleyball was big on the base. It kept the troops amused and out of trouble. Jock's squad had made it into the quarterfinals. This would be their toughest match yet. They had already lost to this same squad two weeks ago, so they were seeking revenge. The challenge was not going to be about talent, but on size. It seemed that the other squad's smallest guy was an even 6 feet tall. Vinnie was the only one on Jock's team standing over 6 feet. They knew that would have to rely heavily on Vin and hope the other side would make some careless mistakes.

Just as the ball left the server's hands, a few drops of rain appeared. This was the first time it rained since the Marines from Parris Island arrived a little more than three weeks ago. There was the occasional early morning drizzle but nothing that was considered an actual rain event. It gave Jock a warm feeling just remembering what it felt like. Nonetheless, they played on knowing they wouldn't have the opportunity to play again because of their deployment orders in just a day and a half. Not more than two minutes later, the rain stopped.

The score stood at 5 to 3 in favor of the squad from Company B. Jock and Vin put their hearts and souls into this match but just couldn't overcome their disadvantages. Time was running out. It was Jock's serve. The serve just missed the top of the net but that didn't stop the opposing team from calling foul. Vinnie had enough. He was at the net when the ball cleared it and could plainly see it miss the net by a good inch. Vinnie could not believe his eyes when the 6-foot 4-inch sandy haired opponent just reached out and grabbed the ball yelling "Net." Vinnie ducked his head under the net and walked over to the guy whining and pushed him flat on his ass. The guy got up and took a swing at Vinnie catching him on the side of the head. Vinnie lowered his stance and charged at his newfound foe tackling him to the ground. By then both sides were going at it. In the middle of things naturally, was Jock. He had already laid out his first confrontation and was working on his next conquest when a small contingent of MPs came swirling out of nowhere with batons in hand and whacking the back of the legs of all those in the scuffle. Getting hit with a baton in the back of the knees immediately sends you to ground. Jock, Vinnie, and the big guy were no different. The officials ruled the game over and awarded Company B squad the winner. It didn't matter too much to Jock, Vin, and the other guys. They seemed to have more fun fighting than playing this game.

Nursing their wounds later that afternoon in the barracks, the squad was in good spirits. Sergeant Shields paid them a visit after he heard of the ruckus from some of the other sergeants on the base. He figured DiNapoli and Donahoe were involved, so he had to go see for himself. Walking into the barracks, he saw Vinnie holding a chunk of ice to the side of his face and Jock wrapping a bandage around his hand.

"Oh shit," murmured Jock, just loud enough for Vin and some of the guys to take notice. Sergeant Shields walked over to Jock first. "I suppose you got your fingernails chipped from playing the piano, hey Donahoe?" Jock got up and stood at attention without saying a word. Then Shields walked up to Vin. "And you, let me guess... you got hit on the side of the head from a copy of the Marine Corps doctrine falling off the top bunk while you were polishing your boots!!" Vin was about to say something but decided to follow Jock's cue of silence.

"Okay, I know who won the game, but I want to know who won the fight?" hollered the sergeant.

"We did," espoused one of the other Marines on the team. "We beat 'em fair and square."

"Outstanding!" said Shields. "That will do as a Christmas gift for this year." Shields exited the barracks not showing the smile growing on his face as he walked out the door.

An announcement was made that the Christmas Day show was cancelled due to the star of the show being AWOL. The good news was that it still would go on but not 'til the next day.

At 0600 hours, the morning of December 26th, reveille was called just like every other day. The swelling had gone down on Vinnie's face, but it still hurt like hell. Jock's bandages were still soaked with blood, and he could hardly even move his fingers. He thought for sure he broke some of them. It took Jock several minutes to unravel the blood-encrusted bandages.

"You better go down to the infirmary and get that hand looked at," said Vinnie.

"I'll be all right, just need a couple of days without any fighting," responded Jock.

"No way, buddy, you gotta get some medical attention and I mean now. If you don't, it ain't gonna heal properly."

"Okay, okay," replied Jock. "I'll go down after we eat."

After their morning rituals, Vinnie got permission to take Jock down to the infirmary to get some x-rays taken of his hand. As they entered the medical station, Jock immediately noticed the young gal he bumped into the first day they arrived. She also noticed Jock and Vinnie. How could anyone not notice the pair? They both looked like they went to hell and back.

"Hi, Monica," said Jock rather meekly. Vinnie gave Jock a nudge forward. "Hello, Private Jock Donahoe and Merry Christmas." Jock returned the formality. "What happened to your hand? And what happened to your friend's face?" They both looked at each other and laughed. "Well, you see we were sort of in this kinda altercation," responded Vinnie. Just then the head nurse came walking up and took over the conversation. "You boys be quiet and listen up. The big one here, go see Nurse Marge over there next to those sinks. You, small fry, follow Nurse Monica over to X-Ray and get that hand scanned." As the head nurse turned and walked away, Jock and Vinnie looked at each other and as though rehearsed, softly said "Merry Christmas to you Nurse Grinch." Monica tried to hide her amusement by looking down at the floor or anywhere but at the two amateur comedians.

Vinnie decided to go over to Nurse Judy instead before the head nurse came back to dish out more verbal abuse. Nurse Judy happened to be a stunning 5-foot 10- inch blonde bombshell with a body that just didn't quit. It took Vinnie no time to make small talk and get her personal information.

While Vinnie was trying to reach first base with Nurse Judy, Monica gingerly placed Jock's injured hand on the x-ray machine plate. Jock tried to mask his facial expressions of pain from Monica, but it was obvious that the hand was broken. "Don't be such a baby" commented Monica with a grin. "Well perhaps if you didn't throw my hand around like it was yesterday's garbage I wouldn't have to wince," retorted Jock. He was getting a little annoyed as Monica's grin grew into an outright smile.

Fifteen minutes later the x-ray was developed. The doctor came over and sat on the stool next to Jock. "Looks like you have a compound fracture of the 5th metacarpal bone of the hand and pisiform bone of the wrist. You will be in a cast for the next four to six weeks Marine." Monica's smile turned to a frown as she overheard the news from twenty feet away as she was attending to another patient. Jock's expression was of disbelief. He never broke anything before and had been in some pretty nasty altercations before. He looked over at Monica. He could see the sadness in her eyes. Jock looked back at the doctor and asked, "Is this going to keep me from shipping out with my battalion?"

"No, I don't think so," responded the doctor. "The fracture is slight, so we will put your hand in a partial cast, and you will just have to try to keep it clean and dry. We'll give you some cotton mittens to help keep the dirt and grime from getting between the cast and your skin."

"That's great, I thought for a moment I was going to miss my all expenses paid luxury cruise to an exotic island." He looked over at Monica again and caught her gazing back. Their eyes locked for what seemed like an eternity. A smile returned to Monica's mouth. Jock was falling for her.

Once the doctor finished setting the cast, Jock went over to find Monica and asked her if she would like to go to the base theater that evening to see the latest films on the war effort. She did not hesitate to say yes.

The cast turned out to be very minimal. It started at his knuckles and ended a few inches past his wrist. He was able to use all his fingers but was uncertain if it would limit his ability to properly sight and shoot his M1 rifle. He guessed he would find out once they were deployed overseas.

The celebrity turned out to be Dorothy Lamoure, the star of stage and screen and still considered available by most accounts. The entire camp went berserk trying to get her autograph or at least get close enough to see her. The lucky ones were able to get their picture taken with her and then get a copy of the photo-op a couple of days later. Jock, Chaz, and Vinnie didn't even bother trying. They were still hung over from the hooch they had back in the barracks after the smoking lamp had gone out.

That evening, Jock met Monica out in front of the base movie tent. Neither of them brought any friends along. "Hello again, Private Jock Donahoe," as she walked up to Jock. Jock had his back to her and didn't notice her walking up until she was just a foot away. He turned quickly startling Monica a bit.

"I'm sorry, I didn't see you," said Jock.

"I'm only glad you didn't whack me with that cast," replied Monica.

"Here, I have something for you." Monica reached into her purse, pulled out a metal object and placed it in Jock's hand.

"What's this?" queried Jock with a slight look of embarrassment on his face.

"It's a pin of Saint Christopher; you know the patron saint of travelers. He will protect you from harm. I figured after your last adventure; you could use all the help you can get." The couple shared a slight chuckle together.

Jock was speechless, but then got up enough nerve to lean over and give Monica a little kiss on her cheek. "Thank you, Monica," he said. "I promise I will take good care of it."

"Well, I was hoping it would take good care of you," replied Monica.

The movie was about to start, and the tent was filling up fast. Jock grabbed Monica's hand and half pulled her to get two seats together. Luckily, there were two unoccupied seats about halfway down on the right. They reached the seats just as two other Marines were approaching, but as soon as the Marines noticed Jock and Monica it was too late.

"Sorry, guys," quipped Jock. The two leathernecks gave a faint nod and continued searching for other seats.

The first few minutes were film clips of the war effort. It was the usual stuff, some actual footage of naval warships pounding some unheard-of island halfway around the globe and the raising of the US flag. Then the feature film started to roll. The crowd got silent. The name of the film was *Above Suspicion*, starring Fred MacMurray and Joan Crawford. It was about an Oxford Professor and his bride. British Intelligence recruited them in 1939 on a spying mission in Nazi Germany. The film just got released two months earlier to the civilian population, so this was the first time being shown at military installations. Monica and Jock settled in and entrenched themselves in the movie.

When the movie ended, the masses of military and civilian personnel exited the quasi-circus tent, except for Monica and Jock. Just when the last of the crowd walked out, Jock turned to Monica and said "I'm shipping out in a few days. I can't tell you where. Hell, I don't know for sure myself, but we think it's an island called Samoa, then on to New Zealand." Monica looked down at her watch, trying to avoid listening to his words. She got up out of her seat, turned away, and started walking down the aisle. Jock gently grabbed her elbow and said "Hey... what gives?"

"Nothing," she responded. "I just don't want to talk about it." Jock was confused but let go of her elbow and followed her outside.

The sky was crystal clear, and it seemed you could see every star in the universe. Monica paused for a moment, turned to face Jock and said "I just have a bad feeling about you, Jock Donahoe. I'm afraid you will not be coming back and there is nothing I can do about it. I feel helpless."

"Don't worry, Monica. I'm not planning on letting any Jap mess with my life."

"How can you say that?" asked Monica in an emotional outburst. "How can you be certain? I've already lost my brother to this war. I don't think I can handle anyone else dying that I have feelings for."

This time Jock grabbed both her hands and said, "Look at me, Monica, look straight into my eyes. I am not going to get killed. This war will end, and I will come home. You just gotta believe." Monica wrestled her hands free and ran, leaving Jock speechless and motionless, just watching her fade away into the darkness, wondering if he would ever see her again.

Chapter IX

The Honeymoon is Over

As it turned out, their shipping orders got changed at the last moment. Their first port of call would be Hawaii. The troops seemed excited; hula girls in bamboo skirts, coconuts, pineapple, and the beautiful beaches and surf that make this island such a paradise. It would take the better of two days to make the trip because of the circuitous route they would have to take to avoid enemy subs.

The convoy full of many fresh and some hardened Marines, along with the necessary essentials to wage war such as ammunition, medicine, and foodstuffs as well as spare parts and tools necessary to repair whatever needed to be repaired embarked from San Diego on the 30th of December 1942. Destination; Honolulu.

Arriving in port late at night on January 1, 1943, dark ominous clouds seemed to have hovered directly over their ships. This actually provided an added security benefit to the activities of the convoy but would cast a pall over the Marines. A torrential downpour would further extinguish any upbeat mood that the Marines had.

Jock and his company were getting edgy of doing nothing but laying in their cots in a makeshift camp situated in a mountainous area about 8 miles outside of Pearl. All they could do was wait for the word to get back on their transports and get into the war. It appeared that there was some sort of FUBAR with logistics. The latest rumor was that the remaining ships that were supposed to arrive days earlier had to take another route because of sightings of Japanese subs in the area. Another rumor had it that some of the ships had to be redeployed to augment the transfer of wounded and sick Marines and soldiers off Guadalcanal.

The letters from home seemed to be arriving less frequently and the troop's attitude was noticeably disconcerting. Everyone was griping about the "hurry up and wait" philosophy. The hurry portion was done. Now they wait.

The next morning, Jock woke up to the shock of cold water

being poured on him. He leaped out of his cot and partially slipped on the wet tarp under him. "Happy Birthday pal." Jock tried to gain his composure only to see Vin and Chaz laughing their asses off.

You sons-of-bitches, you almost drowned me!"

"Stop griping you namby-pamby. It could've been something other than water if you know what I mean," retorted Vin. "Well, you could have at least tried not to get my cast wet. You have no idea how hard it is not to be able to scratch an itch. Anyways, how did you know it's my birthday? I never told anyone."

"We have our ways," said Vin. "We are very resourceful. We are Marines don't forget." The three of them laughed a bit, but Jock was not too happy about the prank.

During breakfast, Vin let on as to how he knew it was Jock's birthday. "You see pal, I told you once that I have this here lady friend that is stationed right here on Pearl. Well, I got together with her the other evening and err, well, one thing led to another and I had her do some snooping through the files on the Sarge and you and a few others. I didn't know you had a punctured eardrum. That's stinks."

"Ya, well that's the way the cookie crumbles. What did you find out about the sergeant?"

"Oh, he's a real hard ass that one. He was headed for officer training school when he got into a scuffle with a couple of NCOs down in New River, North Carolina. It seems that he came to the aid of a young lady and put both those guys in the hospital. One of them filed charges that permanently stained his record. He had two choices, resign his commission, and leave the Corps, or get demoted to corporal and become a Drill Instructor at Parris Island. I guess it wasn't too difficult of a decision hey?"

"That's crap," exclaimed Jock. "Here he does the right thing, and the Corps screws him over."

"Well, that ain't the half of it," replied Vin. "He had to pay restitution to the two guys he kicked the crap out of. It cost him a bundle."

"Remind me when I get my cast off to shake his hand," said Jock. With that said, the two caught up with their other pals down at the canteen for breakfast, then off to target practice.

The good news though was that even with Jock's partial cast, he was able to manipulate pulling the trigger and pulling back on the breach as easily as before his injury. Two and a half more weeks and the cast would come off. Jock could not wait. The itching under the cast was unbearable. He would shove bamboo sticks inside the cast to scratch it. It was just impossible to keep dry especially with this weather. The other good news was that they were shipping out tomorrow, January 3rd. Their destination was still supposed to be classified but it seemed like the entire island knew where they were going.

The rain finally stopped, and the sun made its first appearance on their last day on the island. At least they would be able to dry out their gear. Jock stuck his head out from his tent. For as far as he could see were rows and rows of tents just like his. He was amazed that they could put so many Marines in one confined area and still know where every battalion, company, platoon, and squad were stationed.

The base was abuzz with activity. It felt good to have the sun pelting their exposed skin. It was sort of like a bon voyage message from the heavens. Every single leatherneck was thrilled to finally feel the warm tropical breezes of this small island in the middle of the Pacific Ocean. They expected paradise but not a monsoon. At least for their final day, they would be able to enjoy the true beauty of the island without running for cover.

On January 3rd, 1943, the men of the 2nd Division, 6th Regiment, 3rd Replacement Battalion loaded up on the transport ships along with other war material. It took the entire day to make this happen. The ships were crowded with everything from men, equipment, food, fuel, and other necessities such as medical supplies including plasma. Jock had to be told what the plasma was for. He had no idea.

The flotilla set sail that evening. This was standard operating procedure. It provided an additional level of security that prevented spies from determining exactly the type of ships; how many, and their contents on each of the vessels. It also freed up space at the docks for a long-anticipated convoy of ships coming from the East Coast, through the Panama Canal, and on out to Pearl.

This next leg of the voyage would take nine days which would take them to Samoa. Then, after a day of refueling and unloading some classified supplies, they would continue to their final destination (for another seven days) zigging and zagging to minimize detection from enemy subs. There had been numerous reports that Jap subs had again been seen off the coast of Midway. A loss of one of the transport ships would not only be tragic due to loss of life but would interrupt the dire need for troop replacements all over the Asiatic Pacific theater.

The flotilla consisted of four troop transport ships, each with over 700 men aboard, one hospital ship, two mine sweepers, two ammunition ships, one provisions ship, two destroyer escorts, one landing ship, two submarines and one heavy cruiser. There was also a tender and oilier in with the mix.

Just 100 miles ahead of them was the Carrier Hornet and its battle group that was steaming toward Pago Pago, part of Samoa. It was an instrumental island in the South Pacific for the Navy and Marine Corps. Jock's replacement battalion was on the USS Wharton, which was once a cruise liner converted by the Navy just after the Japs attacked Pearl. It had none of the luxuries of a cruise liner. Just about everything was stripped out but the engine room. This was necessary to make way for heavy equipment, medical supplies and, of course, troops.

Accommodations on the Wharton were cramped at best. Jock got the middle of a three-tiered bunk. Vinnie was on bottom, and their new friend Oscar was on top. Oscar was from Nacogdoches, Texas. He claimed it was the oldest city in Texas. Neither Vinnie nor Jock had any idea, but they liked him, so they never questioned his declaration. Oscar had just turned 19 and was full of vim and vigor. He stood 6 feet tall but weighed only 165 pounds. Still, he was a ferocious scrapper and handled himself very well against his opponents. One time he had to go up against Jock and nearly beat him in hand-to-hand combat training. Jock's saving grace was that Oscar was a little awkward for his size and Jock was able to use his opponent's weight against him. Everybody knew how tough Jock was, so it came as a surprise when Oscar upended Jock more than once. Since then, Oscar, Jock, Chaz, and Vinnie became known as the Four Musketeers in the company. Oscar also taught Vinnie and Jock three-card stud and gave them lessons on playing the harmonica.

As soon as the ship left port, crap games and three card stud were the standard operating procedure. After the third day at sea, the four musketeers were not allowed to play in the same game anymore. Between the four of them, they had pulled in over four hundred and fifty dollars.

Nobody wanted them even to watch from a distance. That was okay with Jock though. He had enough. The smells and the confined quarters were getting to him. He wanted to spend as much time topside as possible.

Day six neared its last few hours of daylight. It was about 1800 hours and the candle lamp would be going out in a few minutes, so Jock and Chaz were having a last smoke at the stern of the ship. Looking out and enjoying the tranquility of calm seas, Jock and Chaz jumped three feet off the deck when the klaxons went off and the announcement "battle stations" reverberated throughout the ship. Within five seconds the antiaircraft guns were rattling away. The noise was deafening.

About four miles off the port side, a single miniscule black dot appeared. It started to grow larger and larger. Then the one object became two. Simultaneously, both objects started to bank, one to the left and the other to the right while gaining altitude. The enemy had at least two aircraft coming directly at their ship. Their orders were simple, find and report the location of the US fleet so their brethren in the Zeros and Kites could unleash their weapons for the sole purpose of sinking as many ships and killing as many of their enemy as possible.

The next thought through everyone's mind was, "Were there more out there?" By this time, the entire convoy was engaged in defensive maneuvers. Smoke filled the air. Every vessel that had armaments was throwing lead into the direction of the oncoming planes.

Just then, there was a huge explosion. A fireball lit the sky and seconds later the remnants of what use to be a Japanese reconnaissance plane fell into the water. The other plane was able to evade the withering barrage of antiaircraft flak and escape the same wrath as his comrade, at least for the moment. Finally, a squadron of HF3 Hellcats came swooping down on the remaining Jap reconnaissance plane and blew it all to hell.

"Whew, that was pretty hairy heh, Jock," remarked Chaz. "It

sure was. I hope they didn't get off a message to their buddies cause if they did, we're gonna have some more excitement that's for sure."

"Well one thing is for certain. The next planes we see will probably be Zeros," chimed Vinnie. The three of them stood quietly, looking out at where the last fireball occurred wondering to themselves when the next engagement might be.

The task force resumed standard operating procedures. A weather pattern was evolving off the starboard bow. Thick, black, ominous clouds were converging on the fleet. You could sense that everyone was tightening up for another miserable ride. Their assumptions did not disappoint. At 0300 the following day, every ship in the task force was slammed around by the almost typhoon-like winds and waves. Even the most stalwart veteran of ocean voyages needed a firm constitution to keep things from getting out of control.

Jock, Vinnie, and Chaz woke up at the same time as everybody else. Several Marines were literally tossed out of their bunks from the roiling waves. A loud crash or two could be heard within the confines of the ship. Evidently, some of the preparations for breakfast met their fate with the deck causing another potentially dangerous situation for whoever crosses this minefield of sorts. Luckily, not very many had any desire for food or drink this morning.

By noontime, the taskforce had sailed out of the worst part of the storm. The ships were still encountering large waves but at least they had a more erythematic pattern, and everybody could roll with the flow. The ocean weary Marines had enough of this sort of torture and just wanted to touch mother earth and go find the enemy. All they had to do was hang in there for another couple of days.

The sudden and vigorous shaking administered by Vinnie caused Jock to jump up and hit his head on the cot above. "Easy there, pal; you're gonna get yourself a purple heart before you even see the enemy," chided Vinnie as Jock rubbed his head.

"What the hell is going on, Vinnie?"

"Just some half naked native gals waving to us that's all."

Jock and Vinnie climbed topside just in time to see their transport ship dock along the wharf in the small harbor. It seemed like every Marine on the ship was already on deck waving back at the natives on the beach. Jock could hardly get a glimpse of the natives of the opposite persuasion causing all the commotion. He was still rubbing his head from the abrupt awakening below deck. "Welcome to Samoa," somebody behind Jock murmured.

When Jock and Vinnie finally disembarked, the native girls were nowhere to be seen. Evidently, the Navy brass got wind of the impending warm welcome and immediately radioed ashore recommending island officials to disperse the welcoming committee. So instead of embracing bare breasted smiling faces, they were greeted with a contingent of grim-faced, gun-toting shore patrol. It sure looked like Samoa was not going to be the paradise they were hoping for. Especially since their stay would be brief.

Other than the beautiful climate and fresh fruit, there was nothing for the Marines to do but rest up and eat. That was okay with most since they were still trying to get their land legs back under them. A day and a half later they were back out to sea on their final leg of their journey.

Early on the morning of January 20, 1943, the task force known as TF 32 had reached their destination, Wellington, New Zealand. The armada had steamed over 5000 thousand miles.

The port in Wellington was picturesque, situated in a relatively large harbor surrounded by rolling hills on one side and the bustling city on the other side. Each pier was jam packed with a variety of ships with merchandise ranging from foodstuffs, military equipment and of course soldiers, many soldiers. The Marines were not the only contingent. Army was there with them.

As it was when they left Pearl, it was standard operating procedure to steam into port during dark. This reduced the risk of the enemy assessing their strengths and weaknesses. By 0400 hours, Jock and the 3rd Replacement Battalion of the 6th Marine Regiment disembarked from the USS Wharton and touched dry land again, well sort of. The wooden wharf seemed to be a mile long, but it didn't matter to the troops. It just felt good. Some of the guys threw themselves down on the pier and kissed the wooden planks regardless that their superior officers almost ripped them a new one for slowing down the line. Almost three weeks at sea, mostly down below in a cargo hold being jostled around by a two-day storm front, not to mention being completely vulnerable when the Jap recon planes spotted the task force, was enough to shake the sturdiest of men. Jock, Vinnie, and the rest of the battalion were glad this leg of the journey was over.

Once all the Marines were off-loaded with their gear, the lead elements including most of the now-empty troop ships left the harbor and set sail for parts unknown. Only a few troop transports, a tender and one light cruiser would stay stationed in port. Jock figured the transports that did set sail again would be used for either sending wounded soldiers back home or for the lead battalion's ticket to their next destination, most likely to the real action. Nobody knew for sure, and nobody was in the mood to find out. All they wanted was a solid footing, real food, and a little sleep without falling out of their cots. The day looked like it was going to be sunny and hot.

Sergeant Shields gathered his platoon and rallied up with Company I of the 3rd Replacement Battalion at 0800. He had just received orders from his Commanding Officer, Captain Faraday, that their next leg of the journey would be by rail car but would have to wait until the rest of the replacement battalions cleared the wharfs.

The sun was just reaching its apex and the troops could feel the strength of its rays right through their khakis. All the troops had finally disembarked, and orders were given to start marching up the main road for about one mile to the rail yard where they would be able to get some chow before boarding the trains.

When the battalions did join up at the train yard, they were greeted by another armed contingent of military police. Their job was to ensure no leathernecks strayed off towards the drinking establishments downtown. They would also be responsible for providing security at the camps. The first thing Vinnie noticed was that the MPs were Army. "Ain't that a horse of a different color."

"Shut your pie-hole, DiNapoli. They are doing their job." Annoyed with DiNapoli as usual, Shields continued directing his men towards the mess tents.

By 14:00 hours, both battalions were waiting for the word to board the trains. Some of the men would get actual seats while others would have to make do in cattle cars, but at least each car was washed down. Sergeant Shields, along with Second Lieutenant

Bates, Lieutenant Blaine, and Captain Faraday were already in the midst of the logistical preparations to board all 720 Marines of the two battalions onto the troop trains awaiting them. The first train could only handle a maximum capacity of 300, so they decided to board as many as they could of 3rd Replacement Battalion onto the first train and let the remaining 60 men or so board the first two cars of the second train. The second train had a few more cars than the first. I Company got to board the second train.

Jock and his fellow I Company Marines clambered aboard the first two cars of the second train only to find out there were no seats. "Holy shit, what are we friggin' cattle?" DiNapoli didn't realize Captain Faraday was right behind him until he heard: "I can always make you run beside the train all the way to the camp, Marine. It's your call." DiNapoli decided to find a spot as far away from Captain Faraday as possible. It was a good decision.

The troops got settled in as much as possible and the trains departed the station. Their top transit speed would be a blistering 20 kilometers per hour. Their destination was a place called McKay's Crossing about 120 kilometers away. An exceptionally long ride when sitting on a wooden floor.

McKay's Crossing was a train terminal situated in a small town called Paekākāriki northeast of Wellington. It was the first major terminal from which all trains continued to Auckland. The US Military had been searching for a large area with relatively flat terrain where troops could be massed right after the Pearl Harbor attack. McKay's Crossing gave them exactly what they were looking for. In fact, the area was large enough for two large camps, one called Camp Russell, the other called Camp McKay. The latter would be home for Jock Donahoe and the two new replacement battalions, along with several other battalions already forming up as replacements to those that died or suffered wounds during the initial Guadalcanal landing and subsequent clean-up operations.

It was just about 19:00 hours when the first train pulled into the station. Although the troops were fed right before they departed the port of Wellington, between the heat and the jouncing up and down on the tracks the troops were famished again and could not wait to get some grub in their bellies. Unfortunately, they were instructed to sit tight until the third train arrived with the remnants of the other battalion. They waited for just over an hour.

When the third train finally arrived, they got the orders to rally over to four makeshift mess halls only 100 meters from the station. Half the troops were tripping over each other just to get in line for the meal, but the MPs made sure things did not get out of hand.

The troops feasted on chicken, or at least it tasted like chicken, and corn bread. It was delicious. For the first time in two weeks, they ate real, fresh food. "I could get used to this," said Vinnie. Jock paused from stuffing his face. "At this moment, I could get use to anything as long as it ain't Spam," then continued to chow down everything on his tin platter.

After their meal, the two battalions were led to their new home about a twenty-minute march from the train station. The camps looked no different than what they had grown accustomed to.

Entering through the main gate where armed MPs were deployed, the Marines mustered in the courtyard. There, they were given their instructions as to the layout of the camp including the locations of the latrines, mess halls, officers' quarters, infirmaries, shelters, and other per functionary facilities one would find in a military installation.

Vinnie, Chaz, and Jock entered their tent of four empty cots close to each other, a small coal- burning stove, and a single bare light bulb dangling overhead. Unfortunately, Oscar was shuffled to another four-man tent, but nobody knew why. There was also one window at the opposite end of the doorway. While the three were unpacking their sea bags, a fourth man came in through the doorway opening. He was a tall lanky kid with red hair and freckles, lots of freckles. Jock figured him to be all of fifteen years of age. "Good day, gents," said the kid as he dumped his sea bag on the floor next to the spare cot. "Hey kid, this ain't no boy scout weenie roast" blurted Vinnie. "Oh, this is where the captain told me what the Namby-Pambies were, so I just wanted to see what one looked like." In an instant, Vinnie had the kid lifted two feet off the ground swearing that he was gonna receive the worst whooping he'll ever encounter. Jock and Chaz had to try everything they could just to get Vinnie to let him go. The kid picked himself up from the floor, brushed himself off and stuck out his hand.

"I'm Owen, Owen P. Chester, the III. I'm from Bowling Green,

Kentucky." The three of them looked at each other in total disbelief. Here stands this skinny, freckled-face kid, who has probably never used a razor in his life, dressed in USMC garb, that came within a hair of getting the daylights kicked out of him. He was still smiling with his hand out to shake the hand of the man who almost conducted the whooping. Jock started laughing first, then the other two followed suit. Pretty soon all four were laughing hysterically. None of them noticed Sergeant Shields standing at the tent opening. "What's all the commotion about!" barked Shields. "Hey Sarge, did you see what the cat dragged in?" Sergeant Shields looked over at the kid, then back at the other three. "This Marine is your new bunk buddy. He will be our radio operator for the company. You will treat him with the utmost respect and protect his ass at all times. Do I make myself clear?" Chaz was the first one to speak up. "But, Sergeant, he can't be all of fifteen."

"I'll be nineteen next month," his smile turning into a snarl that only a mother would think cute.

After a little more lambasting by the sergeant, Vinnie, Chaz, and Jock got the skinny on the new kid. To their amazement, the kid was a whiz with electronics. He received an advanced degree in electrical engineering from Georgia Tech after only two years there. He then immediately joined the Corps and signed up for infantry. The Corps could not dissuade him from this. They even tried to offer him a cushy job with the war department, but he refused. He wanted to be where the action was. He got his wish.

Vinnie finally warmed up to the kid after a couple of days. They just received word that liberty was going to be given out for the weekend. That meant Wellington. That meant bars and broads. Just prior to leaving camp, the men received their pay. That gave Jock fifty-eight dollars on top of the ninety-five he had stashed away from all those poker winnings. Things were looking good.

The train arrived back at Wellington at 1600 hours that Friday. The city was bustling with Marines, Rangers, and Kiwis. Every bar had a line out the door waiting to get in. The first thing Jock, Chaz, Vinnie and their new mascot, Owen, decided to do was to go find a fancy place to eat. They figured there would be plenty of time to drink. "I heard Manning Street is the place to go," chimed in Chaz.

"Ya, that's what I heard also," said Owen. "It's settled then, Manning Street. Now does anybody know how to get there?" The four just looked at each other in silence.

"Why don't we just ask someone," quipped Owen. That instigated Vinnie to give Owen a smack to the back of his head. "Ouch!! What did you do that for Vinnie?"

"We're Marines, you moron. We don't go around asking for assistance. Let's go this way." So, the squad of four maneuvered through the congested streets of downtown Wellington until they found Manning Street.

The roast duck was the best Jock had ever eaten. He could hardly get up out of his chair after the meal. When he did get up, Jock was forced to loosen his belt a few notches. The rest of the guys were in the same state of bliss. None of them felt that they could put away another crumb.

"Whew," said Owen. "That was delicious!"

Then Chaz chimed in, "Kid... the way you put that leg of lamb away, you could probably eat the ass out of a skunk!" The foursome chuckled as they walked out onto Manning Street looking for the nearest pub.

Just across the street was a huge sign that read: Lucky's Saloon. Below the sign were a half dozen Kiwis engaged in a heated debate over a lassie. The four Marines cross the street and cut between the six men still arguing over who had the best chance of getting "on base" with one of the waitresses inside Lucky's. Vinnie made a mental note as to try to find out which broad they were so enamored with.

Walking through the Saloon doors, Chaz noticed the empty table with six chairs way back in the left corner of the bar. He called out to the group saying, "Follow me boys, double-time." The four sat down when Owen remarked, "This is the table those six blokes must have been sitting at."

"Your powers of deductive reasoning never cease to amaze me cowboy," quips Vinnie. Jock and Chaz look at each other and tried not to show their amusement.

Finally, a voluptuous redhead walks over to their table. "What are you going to have yanks?" There was a long pause. The four of them are transfixed on her bosom. Her partially clad attire left very little for the young Marines' imagination and plenty of freedom to foster their own images of what one could do if the opportunity arises.

"Well, boys, I don't have time for you to undress me with your eyes, so tell me what you want to drink."

Vinnie spoke first. "I'll have whatever those six guys that just left here was having." The waitress looked at the other three waiting for their replies, but they were still recovering from the waitress's unabashed statement.

"Come on mates, I ain't got all day."

"Beer... ice cold beer please."

"Yeah," says Owen, "me too"

"That goes for me as well," chimed in Chaz.

The waitress turned to walk away, but then turned back and said, "You Yanks are all alike. Full of vim and vigor, but don't know what to do with it if it landed on your lap."

"Honey, if the rest of the dames are like you, we're gonna win this war in no time," blurted Vinnie. The waitress winked at him and left to fetch their ale. Chaz leaned back in his chair balancing it on two legs, "I'd say you're already on second base Vin."

"Last Call" was the cry out from behind the bar. The four Marines looked at each other. "What the hell, it's only been an hour since we got here," blurted Vinnie. The redhead bounced her way back over to their table. "What will it be boys? The bar closes in five minutes." Vinnie finished his last swig of beer. "But we are only getting started doll."

"Like I said earlier, you Yanks are all the same. Now do you want one more beer before closing or not?" The four nodded in the affirmative.

Owen gulped down the remaining half of his beer and pounded the table with it. "I overheard at the pier that the local government has placed curfews on all drinking establishments and that they can only be open from 1300 to 1700 hours. This way they could keep us from getting stinking drunk late at night, and Australian gals could get back to their husbands and boyfriends in time for dinner."

"Well, don't that beat all. What, are they afraid we're gonna just love 'em and leave 'em?"

"Not likely Vinnie. I think they're afraid that we will leave their town without a drop of booze left."

Luckily, Owen had purchased a fifth of scotch earlier in the day while on their way to dinner. This brought smiles to the other three as they passed around the bottle until it was empty.

It was 1845 hours and the four Marines had to hightail it back to the station if they were going to make the last train back to camp. If they didn't make it, all hell would break loose, and they would be thrown in the brig for a day or two losing their privilege of getting another liberty pass for weeks. That was incentive enough for the four of them to pick up the pace.

Running down the street as fast as they could, it looked more like a stampede that just a few guys trying to catch a train. There must have been a hundred Marines, most of them stumbling their way back to reach the last train to camp.

Right on cue, the train blew its whistle and slowly began to chug away from the station. The last one on was Owen, and he needed help. The other three had to jump on first and pull him up and onto the last car. Owen turned around to see the station disappear from sight and puked over the railing onto the tracks. The ride back to camp consisted of mostly snoring from drunken Marines.

Chapter X

Tell Dad Not to Worry

For the next few days, the two new replacement battalions got officially merged into the different regiments. Jock's battalion became 3rd Battalion, 6th Marine Regiment commanded by Colonel Maurice G. Holmes. Their Battalion Commander was Lt. Colonel Kenneth McLeod. The other battalion became part of the 2nd Marine Regiment under Colonel David M. Shoup. Once the formalities were set, new training exercises were scheduled. This time they would conduct extensive amphibious assault tactics at Hawkes Bay.

Sergeant Shields and about a hundred other NCOs and lieutenants got their briefing on the upcoming exercises in the Planning and Logistics tent. Actually, it was four huge tents patched together. It gave enough room to hold over two hundred personnel with charts and plans and communication equipment.

After the Brass completed their dissertation, the floor was opened up for any comments or suggestions. Naturally, Sergeant Shields was curious about the tides and the shoreline. From what he could gather, the landing zone had no protection from the onslaught of waves. On one side, no more than one thousand feet to the left was a sheer rock cliff over 100 feet high. On the other side was nothing but ocean. He was really concerned about how the waves would break so near the craggy rock formations.

"Sir, has the tide been taken into account for tomorrow morning?" A captain stood up from the same table where the upper Brass were sitting at and replied, "Of course it has Sergeant. We have been over this with our climatologist. No unusual weather patterns are predicted for another two weeks." Shields was not convinced. "How about confirming this forecast with some of the locals? They would surely know this area better than any outsider." The captain was getting a little annoyed with him now. "Now look here, Sergeant, your concerns are justified, but that is why we have our own specialist. We don't like taking anything to chance." Shields sat down knowing he was not going to get the answer he was looking for.

The call to reveille doesn't change much from nation to nation. The only difference was the notes and the instrument being used. In this case, the Marines did not wake up to the loud bugle call associated with their training back in the States but were greeted by Sergeants entering each encampment hollering to get their tails in gear or suffer the consequences. The sound of dozens of Sergeants delivering their own personal message to the troops felt really strange to the Marines, but it didn't stop them from following standard operating procedure; "Hurry up and wait."

By 05:50 hours, the Marines were at attention waiting for their day to begin. Shields looked up into the sky and noted the fast-moving dark gray cumulus clouds. He had an ominous feeling in his gut.

Sergeant Shields, along with Second Lieutenant Bates briefed their platoon on this morning's training exercise. Then Captain Faraday gave his little gung-ho speech and nodded to Shields to saddle up.

During chow, Vinnie was able to glean a little more intel from Shields while filling his mouth with oatmeal. Shields took Vinnie aside and told him to keep the platoon as close together as possible when hitting the beach. He was concerned that the surf would be rough. "But, Sarge, aren't we supposed to spread out, so we all don't make like a huge single target?"

He grabbed Vinnie's right arm. "Look, just do what I tell you." Vinnie did not say another word and went back to his table to fill in the other guys.

Their first amphibious practice landings were to take place on the Paekākāriki coast near Wellington. The Marine units loaded up their gear onto the Deuce-and-a-halfs for their trip back down to the wharfs. From there, they would board some makeshift transport ships and sail down and around Wellington and up the west coast to Paekākāriki.

At 0800 the two battalions conducted the first of three practice landings. Fortunately, the weather was participating for the time being. The low cloud cover moved off leaving plenty of sun and a light breeze. Sergeant Shields' gut feeling was all for naught. Other than one Higgins boat getting caught up on a sand bar, the entire exercise went off without a hitch.

Lighting up a Chesterfield enroute back to Camp McKay, Vinnie took a deep draw of the cigarette. "Well fellas, I guess the Sarge is turning into a worry- wort."

"Give me one of those will ya." Vinnie handed Jock a Chesterfield and struck a match for him also. "Well Vinnie, I'd rather be wrong than dead." Chaz grabbed the cig out of Jock's mouth and took a long haul. "If it was up to me, I would always go with my gut instinct first."

Sergeant Shields rounded the back end of the truck and heard Chaz's last comment. "What gut instinct would that be?"

"Oh, we were just talking about that feeling you get in the pit of your stomach right before you are about to do something that you would not normally do," replied Vinnie. "Yeah, well I still feel we dodged a bullet today. Now get rid of the butts cuz we're headed back to camp. Tomorrow is gonna be another swell day."

That evening, Jock's platoon got the skinny on the rest of the week's training exercises which would consist of marching, and then march some more. The field march would consist of the entire regiment in the bush for three days.

The terrain was mostly rolling hills north of Camp McKay. The purpose of all the marching was to keep the Marines in tip-top shape in the event they were needed for combat operations sooner than anticipated. It also got them acclimated to the high humidity.

At the end of the three-day exercise, the battalion nursed swollen ankles, blisters, and a few nasty infections from some sort of insect bite. No one knew for sure just what the hell caused the circular ring with a dark spot in the middle. All they knew is that it itched like poison ivy but then it would disappear after a day or two. The sore would form into a pimple-like head and eventually ooze out puss, then leave no tell-tale scar or mark. Nobody suffered any life-threatening conditions from it other than being the recipient of a few embarrassing jokes.

During the evening most of the Marines would write to their loved ones back home. Jock wrote his letter to his younger brother who was a senior in high school.

"Hi, Bob, Hope this letter finds you well. How are sis and father? I have not received any mail since we left the mainland. Perhaps Uncle Sam just

has not caught up with us yet. How is school? It is hard to believe you will be graduating in May. Have you decided what you are going to do when you get out? Think really hard about it and don't make any rash decisions. All I can tell you is that I am in New Zealand, but I cannot say exact location. Its hot down here considering the time of year. Their summers are our winters. It's crazy. I've made some swell pals down here and most have been with me since boot camp. They all think I talk funny because of my Boston accent. Got to keep this short for the war effort and all. The smoking lamp goes out in a minute anyway.
P.S. Tell Dad not to worry.
Your big brother

Just as Jock was folding the V mail letter into the small envelope, he hears some of the guys talking that the battalion may be getting new orders very soon and will be shipping out. Jock realizes most of these persistent rumors and scuttlebutt never come to reality, so he just shrugs it off and puts the letter away until he gets a chance to mail it within the next day or so.

The following morning to everyone's surprise, the entire battalion is informed that they are getting a reprieve from any additional intensive training or exercises for the next four days. With this unsuspected liberty, the Marines scattered to the four winds of the island. Jock, Vinnie, Chaz, and Owen shared a hotel room in downtown Wellington for the entire time taking frequent trips and exploring the lush countryside. It also meant booze, butts, and broads. It appeared that the last thing on their minds was the war.

Wellington could accommodate large numbers of troops. It had to. Many of the hospital ships and troop transports and assorted destroyers made this city home. So, Wellington officials did everything they could to welcome the injured and the sick and those being readied to go off to fight. It was also the host for the largest mortuary in the Pacific theater. What seemed like almost daily, dead soldiers from every allied nation were processed through here. During some of the fiercer campaigns, it got to be such a high casualty rate that the US Military had to start conducting funeral and burial services out at sea. This was the only way to keep the ships from getting overburdened, minimize diseases, and free up critical space for war effort material.

On their last day of liberty, the four Marines frequented their favorite watering hole back down on Manners Street and, as was the custom, at 1700 hundred hours they would be pushed out onto the streets where they would continue their little party until passing out or finding other forms of entertainment or wind up in the brig for the evening.

Vinnie could drink enough for two without any noticeable diminishing quality in his speech. Jock, on the other hand, would slur his words after four beers. This time a contingent of Kiwis was walking by when one of them thought they heard Jock say, "Let's fetch some fast dames." The Kiwi put his hand up halting the other guys in the group, and then walked over to Jock. "I say yank, what in the blazes did I hear you say?" Jock had to look up to the man. He was at least 4 inches taller and 40 pounds heavier. "Wut I juz sed is of no concern of yaws mate."

The guys from each crew quickly lined up next to Jock and the Kiwi, waiting for someone's next move. The Kiwi grinned and said, "Now look here peewee, it is a concern of mine if you go around insulting our lasses."

"First, if you call me peewee once more, I'll knock ya teeth down ya throat. Second, I did not say anything that was insulting to you or the women that live here." The Aussie's jaw dropped a bit not expecting such an aggressive response from the diminutive Marine. "Well, tough guy, it sure sounded to me that you said, "Let's catch some fast dames."

Vinnie stepped up between the two to defuse the escalating confrontation. He said, "Let's catch the next train." The Australian soldier and his buddies looked at each other. "Well, why didn't your buddy just say that?" Vinnie looked back at Jock, then turned back to the Kiwis and said "My buddy had a little too much to drink and slurs his words a bit. No harm done my friends. Let's not get your skivvies all knotted up over some mispronounced words, okay?" Jock had already sized up the odds and was all set for battle just waiting for someone to make the first move towards him. But the Kiwis decided not to pursue any further. "Just get your intoxicated little friend back to his base before he opens his trap again." Jock was about to respond but felt a hand grab the back of his belt. It was Chaz standing beside him trying to implement some restraint.

The Kiwis walked off making some sort of negative gesture in their departure. Vinnie Chaz, Jock and Owen breathed a quiet sigh of relief. None of them feared the confrontation. They feared what Shields would do if he found out they got into another fight.

The following day, word got out that there was a bloody riot down on Manners Street between US Marines and Australian soldiers. Several men on both sides were seriously injured and dozens were thrown in brigs awaiting disciplinary action .

When Jock and Vinnie found out, Jock gave Vinnie a grateful nod intended to show his appreciation from pulling him out of an undesirable situation. Vinnie nodded back. There was no need for words.

Once back at camp, Jock pulled out all his letters from home and read each one over and over. He then realized he never sent the letter he wrote to his brother just before liberty was given.

Vinnie came over as Jock was refolding all his mail and stuffing them back into their envelopes before putting them back in his footlocker. He kept the letter to his brother on the bunk. "Hey Jocko, why don't you and me go down to the camp PX and pick up a couple of sodas."

"Sure, why not. I can mail this letter that I forgot all about on the way."

Coming out of the PX, they bumped into Second Lieutenant Bates. Giving them the once over and noticing Jock was without his cast, he asked "How's the hand, Donahoe?"

"Fine, LT. Can't even tell it was ever broken. The best part of all, I get to scratch any time I want to now." Bates looked at Jock squarely in the eyes. "You are gonna need both hands when it comes to the real action so don't go getting into anymore altercations."

"Sir, the only altercations I'll be getting into is with the Japs."

Vinnie nudges Jocko. "Don't you have a letter to mail?"

"Oh... right, later, Lieutenant."

About twenty feet after departing the lieutenant, Jocko says, "What's the deal, Vin?"

"I just don't like the guy that's all. He's a creep. I think he reports everything to the captain."

Jock puts his hand on Vin's shoulder. "You don't like anyone, do you?"

"I like you and Shields, that's it. You two are the only ones I trust with my life. If I have to share my foxhole with anyone it would be you or Shields." Jock drops his letter off at the mail tent, and they walk back to their tent pushing each other trying to make the other trip from time to time.

Chapter XI

Itching for Action

On the morning of February 1st, Jock's battalion got the word that they were shipping out to a place called Russell Island. Again, most of them never heard of Russell Island. It was a small island just a mile or so Southwest of Guadalcanal. It was more of an atoll than anything else, but from here they could stage their operations prior to being ferried over to Guadalcanal.

Although the major fighting had ended months ago during the Guadalcanal campaign, there were still a few enemy stragglers that refused to give up and harassed the Seabees trying to rebuild the landing strip and fortify the island. Jock's battalion would provide protection for the Seabees and to root out any remaining enemy.

One week after landing on Russell Island, Jock noticed he was losing his appetite. He was quickly diagnosed with malaria like symptoms and was immediately treated with quinine. Though this helped get his appetite back, he began to get sores in his mouth and gums. After one month on the island, he started to lose some of his teeth. The infirmary increased the dosage of the quinine and after another few days the sores and gum pain dissipated. None of his other buddies seemed to be affected but there were reports that out of the 720 Marines that arrived on the island, forty of them were sent back to Wellington and another forty, along with Jock, were diagnosed with the early stages of malaria but were still fit for active service. Over the following several weeks, more than thirty additional Marines came down with malaria or other island diseases. Since Jock was able to hold down his food and perform his duties, he was not considered unfit for duty. So, he trudged along in the Marine corps tradition routine day to day.

These next two months proved to be monotonous and boring. All they did was provide security details during the loading and off-loading of supplies from ship to shore and vice-versa. Most of the supplies consisted of dry goods, fuel, and drugs such as morphine, quinine, sulfa, and salt pills.

Russell Island became a huge supply depot. It had its own airstrip and was very close to Guadalcanal with its expanded runway so it provided an ideal situation for resupplying the war effort as it was never really occupied by the Japs other than a small token force. Therefore, it was thought to be the most secure in terms of keeping the enemy from finding out about the supplies and logistical support apparatus.

Jock's platoon was given the transport detail. This encompassed driving the fully loaded Deuce-and-a-half from the pier to the supply depot located about a half mile inland.

About one click in from the pier, Jock felt the steering well pull to the right and shake violently. "Hey, what the cripes are you doing Jocko?" yelled Vinnie sitting in the co-pilot's seat. "I'm trying to keep the friggin' truck on the road. I must have a blow out or something. The rest of the vehicles behind Jock and Vinnie come to a screeching halt also. Some of the drivers laid on their horns. "Pipe down, you horses' asses… pipe down," hollered Vinnie as they both got out to check the tire.

They were expecting to find a good ole- fashioned flat tire but to their astonishment, the entire tire and wheel were missing from the front axle. "Holy shit! How the hell did that happen?" The guys from the truck behind them walked up. "Hey, Donahoe, where the hell did you get your license from… Sears and Roebucks? The two chuckled while Jock and Vinnie were still scratching their heads trying to figure out how the wheel came off and where it could be. "Seems like everywhere I go with you Jocko we end up in a ditch. First the bus ride from Trenton to Philly, now this. Damn, we are friggin' lucky we didn't flip over and mess up your hair."

Once the laughter subsided, the Marine driving the truck behind them points to the bushes to their right. "You might want to take a look in there. I believe something belongs to you." Vinnie hacks away the bush with his rifle and hits a solid object. He clears away a little more and finds the tire and wheel still intact. "That's odd. It looks like it is in perfectly good shape." Vinnie pulls the tire out and rolls it over to the right front axle. "All we need now are some lugs. Any suggestions?" Jock rounds the back end of the truck and crawls under the chassis to where the spare tire is mounted. "Son of a bitch" roars Jock. "Not only are there no spare lugs, but there is no spare tire either!"

As Jock is climbing out from under the truck the NCO arrives with a look of disgust on his face. "What the hell did you stop for Marine? We have got to get these supplies to the depot before dusk and you are mucking up the whole works!"

"Sir, we lost a tire, and we have no means of repairing or replacing it."

"Then I suggest you high tail it back to the pier and find the necessary supplies to get it fixed... and I mean right now!"

"Yes, sir." Vinnie and Jock started jogging back to the pier as the remainder of the convoy moved out, all leering at the two that caused the disruption.

Back at the pier, the two caught up with Sergeant Shields and Second Lieutenant Bates. They briefed them on their dilemma and were able to acquire the necessary pieces, get a ride back to their disabled vehicle, and put the vehicle back in operational status. By this time, the sun was just setting, and they were still about 2 clicks out from the depot. They both knew that they would miss chow, but that would not be their only misfortune this day.

Arriving at the entrance to the supply terminal, two large and very mean looking Marines pointed their rifles at the windshield of the truck. "Hey, guys, easy does it, will ya?" exhorted Vinnie as he climbed down from the rig.

"Do not take another step or I will fire."

"Whoa, buddy, we're on your side. Now just point that thing in another direction." The sentry refused to comply.

Out from behind the sentry shack came a pudgy, red-faced junior officer sweating profusely. You could tell he was still chewing on something because it took him a moment to speak. "Stand down, sentry." The sentry obliged.

"Thanks, sir. He was scaring the bejeezus out of me."

"And rightly so. He was performing his duty and following orders. No vehicles of any kind are allowed to enter this depot after 1800 hours. It is now 1820." Jock explained their ordeal, but it fell on deaf ears.

As the junior officer was finishing telling Jock and Vin to go back where they came from, another officer showed up. "Is that you, Donahoe?"

Jock turned around to see Captain Faraday. "Yes, sir, hello, Captain Faraday."

"What is all the fracas about, son?" Jock explained the whole thing again, right down to the missing lug nuts.

"Let this vehicle through, Lieutenant." The portly officer was flabbergasted but did what he was told and allowed Jock and Vinnie through.

"Thanks, Captain." Vinnie jumped back in and as they drove by the irritated officer, he winked at him causing the red-faced man to turn a deeper shade of purple. "It's nice to have friends in high places, Jocko. Now let's find our platoon."

At 1845 hours, Vinnie and Jock were in their platoon's makeshift barracks in the northeast sector of the depot. Most of the platoon razzed the two for the rest of the evening. At least they would be able to sleep in the relative comfort of cots and a tent versus the confines of the front seat of the truck.

Come mid-April, Jock's battalion got a reprieve from their security detail and was shipped back to Wellington for some additional training and rest. The other battalion was ordered to stay put. This was fine with Jock and the gang. He had lost several teeth by now and was having difficulty chewing anything solid. But at least he was feeling better, and the steely blue color came back to his eyes. The first thing Jock was going to do was visit the infirmary to see if they could make up some false teeth. He was anxious to chew on a real piece of meat again, even if it was kangaroo meat. It wasn't that it tasted any different than cattle from home; it was just the thought of it that gave Jock a little queasiness.

About three weeks later, a dentist was able to fit Jock with some upper dentures. The lowers would have to wait due to his condition not being as severe as many other Marines requiring major orthodontic surgery. For the most part, Jock was able to chew fish and boiled chicken. The beef would have to wait.

One evening in June of 43, while Jock's company enjoyed R & R, Sergeant Shields entered the base recreation center where Jock, Vinnie, Chaz, and Owen were drinking some warm beer and playing cards.

A greeting of "Hello, Sarge" came from all four simultaneously. Shields looked directly at them all without saying a word. Vinnie was the first to chime in. "What's the matter, Sarge?" Sergeant Shields grabbed a stool leaning against the tent pole and straddled it backwards. "I just got word that several Marines died earlier today off the coast of Paekākāriki in Hawkes Bay."

"What? How did it happen?" queried Jock.

"Just like I was afraid it would happen, but the sonsofbitches didn't listen to me. It seems that Marine units of the 2nd Marine Regiment were engaged in practiced landings exactly where we conducted those same exercises months ago. But this time disaster struck. At about 2030 hours last night, the weather deteriorated and one of the landing boats got grounded on a sandbar. Then without any warning whatsoever, a huge wave swamped it. The men were thrown into the heavy surf. Luckily, there were other landing craft in the area that was able to pull out some survivors, but it was dark. It appears they lost 20 Marines in an instant."

The guys just sat there, frozen to every word Shields spoke. Shields got up and walked out. The guys knew what was going through his mind. He was blaming himself for not pursuing his gut instinct by going higher up on the chain of command. Jock got up and followed Shields out the door to try to console him.

"Hey, Sarge, wait up." Shields didn't slow down so Jock had to pick up his pace a bit. "Are you all right, Sarge?"

"No.... no, I'm not all right, Donahoe. Just let this be a lesson to us all. Even the ones with the brass on their shoulders are human. No man should play God with other men's lives.... No one!" Jock placed his left hand on the sergeant's right shoulder and said "That's why God made Marine Corps Sergeants. To keep the Brass from making fools of themselves all the time." Shields looked into Jock's eyes. "There's gonna be a time when I'm not there, kid. Just remember that." Shields gave Jocko a grin and a wink and walked away.

Rested and back in almost perfect health, Jock's battalion along with the other replacement battalion still serving on Russell Island were shipped off to the chain of islands known as New Guinea. The date was August 22, 1943. Their mission was to replace a battered division of Army Infantry that had seen action in the city of Salamaua. From there, they would conduct a series of campaigns to root out Japanese strongholds in the interior of the island.

The two Marine battalions along with elements of US Army Infantry and Australian Marine units hopped from island to island known as Baker Island, Arundel Island, and Choiseul. Limited action was seen, but it got them their first taste of sleeping with one eye open. There were a few instances where a Marine was missing from their position, only to then be found with his neck sliced or hanging from a palm tree by his ankle with a long spear piercing completely through his body.

The Marines were not taking anything to chance. Prior to landing on each island, the Division would receive word from the 'coastwatchers' regarding enemy activity. In addition to that, advanced scouting teams would come ashore at night to recon. Only at Choiseul did the Marines encounter a small contingent of Japanese Imperial Marines. But they choose to circumnavigate the small force knowing that they posed no strategic threat to their operational plans. In fact, it lent the impression that the US Marines were establishing a permanent base on the island when instead it was being used as a feint for their ultimate goal; the amphibious landing at Tarawa atoll on Betio.

On October 10th, they left Choiseul to go back to Wellington to link up with other elements of the 2nd Marine Division, more specifically the 2nd and 8th Marine Regiments in preparation for the Tarawa Invasion.

The operation, known as 'Operation Galvanic' was shrouded in complete secrecy. The Marines thought they were going to Hawkes Bay, the site where most amphibious exercises were conducted. A rumor was started that the troops would be back in Wellington in time for a scheduled social event with their Australian counterparts. Instead, the three Marine regiments joined up with Admiral Hill's Southern Attack Force at Efate Island located in the New Hebrides. Here the Marines rehearsed their amphibious assaults with every variety of craft available to the Marine corps. including light and medium duty tanks.

In the rehearsals, live ordinance was used on some of the less inhabited islands such as Erradaka Island. This gave the Marines a more realistic urgency as to the impending invasion.

The exercise was so big that two days later, Tokyo Rose was making it well known via the airwaves that the Japanese Imperial Marines knew of their preparations to invade somewhere, and that they were ready for any invasion the US Marines could muster. They just didn't know where.

A few days later, the US forces learned that the Japanese commander defending Tarawa boasted to his men that "Not a million men could take this island in a thousand years." The challenge was accepted by the US Marines.

On November 1, 1943, Task Force 53 left Wellington towards Tarawa, which was an atoll that formed a portion of the Island known as Betio, one of the islands in a chain known as the Gilbert Islands.

Chapter XII

You Can't Live Forever

In the predawn light of November 18th, the silhouettes of each ship could just be made out by the naked eye. The view was awe inspiring. Jock, Vinnie, and the gang were looking off the starboard side of their troop transport ship. What they saw was an array of ships totaling more than 200. From their vantage point, Jock could make out carriers, battleships, cruisers, and destroyers. Off to the port side were dozens of troop transports just like theirs. "There must be a million men on these ships," cried Owen. Right on cue, Vinnie gave Owen the usual slap on the back of his head. Owen had become accustomed to it.

Climbing down from the forecastle, Sergeant Shields and Second Lieutenant Bates met up with I Company of the 3/6. The look in Shields' eyes seem to give away his mood, while Bates on the other hand was evidently very agitated. Vinnie keenly noticed the difference between the two. "What gives, LT?" Bates started kicking at the cargo holds topside. "We have been assigned as the reserve unit." Jock couldn't believe what he just heard. "What? How come, Lieutenant? Hell, we've been the ones given the most training! Why are they holding us back?" The sergeant stepped out from behind Bates to calm Jock down. "'Cause they are saving the best for last.... that's why Donahoe, so don't be in such a dam hurry to get shot at. You'll get your chance." The rest of the guys espouse the same response as Donahoe. Shields has to tell them all to pipe down.

Vinnie puts his big hands on Jock's shoulders. "Come on, buddy, the sarge is right. Maybe they got bigger plans for us." Jock turned around to face Vinnie. "Yeah, like providing security for k-rations and toilet paper. I didn't join the Marines to play babysitter."

"Knock it off, Donahoe. These are our orders. We will remain onboard until such time we are given an assignment. Until that time, watch and enjoy the fireworks." It was evident that Bates didn't like the orders he was given also. He walked off leaving Shields to complete the briefing to the rest of the company as to their involvement.

Jock sat in his bunk looking distraught. He was tired of all the training, and then moving about from camp to camp, and then waiting for something to happen. Finally, when his chance to really get into the fight and give those Jap bastards a taste of good ole American revenge for Pearl Harbor his battalion is placed in reserve. The more he thought about it, the more agitated he became.

Later that evening, the actual invasion plans were distributed to each regiment, battalion, and company. The transports arrived off Tarawa just after midnight on November 20th. The plan was for aircraft from the carriers to initiate the strike at 0545 hours. Then the big guns of the US Navy would pound the island for two hours with the planes returning for a final strafing run five minutes before the first assault waves land. Everyone knew their part. The lessons learned from the Guadalcanal campaign were well entrenched in the minds of the veterans that participated. It was only if the situation warranted that the 3/6 would be called in as a reserve battalion. Otherwise, they would watch from the confines of their troopship as other elements of the amphibious assault force would make history, one way or the other.

Unfortunately, none of this went according to plan. At 0507 hours, alerted by the pre-dawn activities of the US Armed Forces, the Japanese initiated the first strike by opening fire with their big guns. Within a minute, the main batteries of the USS Maryland and Colorado returned fire. By the Japanese initiating the first volley, this gave the Navy a confirmation as to the location of the island gun defenses and within minutes several 16-inch shells from the two battleships made a direct hit on an ammunition bunker adjacent to one of the island guns. A huge fireball erupted lighting the entire sky. This gave the impression to the US Forces that there would be no need to continue the naval bombardment figuring the naval aviators could finish things off. But the carrier group changed their plans and postponed the aerial bombardment by thirty minutes. This provided the Japanese some precious time to recover from the initial artillery barrage and reposition their defenses for the actual amphibious invasion.

At 0605 hours the guns of Task Force 53 resumed firing. At 0610 hours, aircraft from the carriers appeared so all ship firing had to be silenced once again. Amid all this confusion it was noted that the sun rose an ominous blood red color.

The roar of the big guns and the buzz of the fighter planes overhead ensured that everyone had woken up from their slumber. They could even feel the vibration of the mighty battleships and cruisers that were several miles away as they delivered their wake-up call to the enemy. "Jesus, do you hear that?" Chaz cupped his hands over his ears. "Hear it, I can friggin feel it!" screamed Vinnie just to make sure Chaz could hear him. "Are we sure we're not the ones getting clobbered?"

After the initial engagement, the men from the 3/6 could hear Marine Corsairs and Hellcats fly over their troopship enroute to cover the amphibious assault teams. It did not take long for the scuttlebutt to get back to the ships that the first wave of Marines was having a hard time crossing the coral reef in the Amtracs and that the pounding the island took from all the warships was basically ineffective. Observers had noted that several rounds had skipped across the narrow island and landed in the water on the other side.

By dusk on D-Day, it was evident that the enemy was not going to give up this tiny atoll. Casualties were high; several amphibious vehicles were destroyed or damaged, and communications on the command nets were sporadic at best. No one on the flagship really had a concise picture of what was happening on the beaches. One thing they did know; not one landing craft was able to cross the reef during the entire D-Day. The men had to jump over the gunwales and slog the remaining distance of 500 to 1000 yards suffering the full enfilading fire from the Japanese. The planners did not heed the islanders warning of a "dodging tide."

Later that evening, Shields had come back down with his men to give them an update. "We have new orders." Pausing long enough to make sure everyone could gather round. "The 3/6 is getting their chance. We will participate in the landing of Tarawa. We are to be prepared to embark within the next 24 hours. Our objective is to rendezvous with the 1st Battalion, 6th Marines on Beach Black and be prepared to support them in resisting Jap counterattacks. Until then, we sit tight."

The men looked at each other. Some with grins, others with looks of bewilderment. Chaz was nearest to Sergeant Shields as the entire group started talking over each other to try to figure out what was really going on. "What's changed Sarge?" The sergeant placed his right foot on a small wooden crate labeled First Aid and scratched his head. "Radio messages from the beach have been few and disrupted, but from what command can piece together, it appears that the first three waves have encountered unusually heavy opposition with casualties as high as 70 percent. Another message stated, "Can't hold, request reserve units." There was an eerie silence for a moment. As Chaz was stuffing an extra pair of clean socks into his pack his jaw dropped. "Holy Shit, I thought with the tons of shells we unleashed on those bastards, they would have swum back to Japan!"

"Well, they didn't and they sure as hell ain't gonna leave even if we ask them pretty please! So, I suggest that all of you triple check your gear now cause you ain't gonna have time to check it later. I'll let you know when we disembark as soon as someone tells me."

Shields's steely gaze pierced each and every soldier's eyes. The look of anxiety in each Marine's face could not be more obvious. There was silence again, and then the men started their perfunctory routine of addressing the sergeant's suggestion.

After Shields left, Owen joined up with Jock, Vinnie, and Chaz. "Where have you been?"

"I was topside having a cig when I overheard some scuttlebutt." Vinnie squeezes his big hand tightly around the back of Owen's neck. "Well, are you going to tell us?"

"Okay... okay, I was about to. It seems that one of the LVTs returned back to the transport Zeilin with no one at the controls. All they found were two dead Marines and a dead navy medic." Vinnie let go of the grip he had around his neck.

On the morning of November 22, D+2, the Marines of the 3/6 commanded by Lieutenant Colonel Kenneth F. McLeod climbed down the cargo nets of the USS Harris. Jock's battalion had performed this exercise several times now, but it didn't get any easier. There were just too many variables such as wind, rain, wave height, time of day, not to mention drawing enemy fire that even under the ideal conditions was dangerous at best. At least they would be getting a ride in the updated version of landing craft affectionately known as the Water Buffalo. It was technically the LVT 2 which was built to improve on the shortcomings of the earlier version LVT 1. This was done by adding additional armor, more horsepower, and rubber tires. But it still lacked one thing; there was no ramp. The men still had to unload off the gunwales.

It was almost 0600 hours and peering over the top of the LVT Jock could make out what appeared to be sporadic sheets of flames and thick black smoke all along the Southern shoreline. It looked like the entire island was engulfed in flames. Meanwhile, if the Marines weren't sickly white from the bobbing up and down of the landing craft, then that was because they were overcome with terror.

Every few minutes or so a mortar shell or cannon fire would come dangerously close to the landing craft breaking the Marine's concentration of just not embarrassing themselves until they hit the beach. The enemy salvos were of less frequency than the day before, but more accurate. This did not inspire much confidence between the Marines and the Navy.

They were now just 2000 yards from the beach and waiting at the line of departure for the orders to be given by the Wave Commanders to advance. Their wait was short. At 0700 the remnants of craft that survived the initial assaults over the last two days were now pressed into action. The motors on the crafts revved up in unison belching its own thick black smoke as they headed for Beach Black #2 in an open 'V' formation. "Here we go" yelled out an unknown Marine standing forward in the LVT. All around Jock were men whispering their prayers or just holding on to their rifles as tightly as possible. The closer the boats got to the beach the more salvos of enemy fire rained down on them.

After what seemed like several hours, the coxswain yelled out "This is it, over the sides," and with the assistance of two naval personnel to pass over supplies the men jumped down into the water.

Gathering their equilibrium in the shifting sands and loose coral beneath their feet the Marines hesitated for a second, noticing they must still be at least 300 yards from shore. Then the officer leading the squad yells out "Let's move it, you can't live forever!"

Jock was in water up to his neck as he plied over the side of the LVT. Over half of the guys lost their footing and were totally immersed. "Jesus H. Christ," yelled one of the Marines. "Couldn't the

Navy get us in a little closer?"

Just 200 yards to land, geysers of water would erupt around the reserve units. "Mortar fire. Let's move it!" screamed the squad officer. Then, in a blink of an eye, a large plume of red droplets fell on the Marines. Their leader was gone. The mortar round must have hit him directly on the head. The unit kept moving towards shore. Jock waded by a couple of dead Marines floating face first in the water. He tried not to look down at the corpses to see if he would recognize any of them. It would have been difficult to because their bodies were bloated from the seawater and sun. In fact, the bodies were already decomposing, and the odor was inescapable. Finally, a voice from directly behind him brought him back to reality. "Get moving Marine or you'll end up like them." Jock didn't know who said it but heeded the advice and slogged towards the beach, his rifle now in a position which he could use without it getting water-logged and unable to fire.

Although the beach head had been established for the last 36 hours and the Marines entrenched, their position was tenuous at best. The Japs would counter-attack in suicidal waves. The enemy mortar fire did not let up. Every time the Japs shot some off, they would quickly pack up and relocate to another designated location and popped off some more.

Upon reaching shore, Jock and the other Marines had to crouch low and run towards the leading forces makeshift fortification that consisted of trenches, logs, debris, and the occasional burnt-out hulk of a tank or Amtrac. In his haste to make a beeline to safer ground, Jock looked around to see if he could identify his buddies that were arriving on another LVT, but there was just too much confusion.

There was sporadic enemy gunfire directed at the unit as they moved in off the beach. Logistical support apparatus could not be unloaded because of the intense counter attacks and mortar fire. The landing zones had to be kept clear for the assault units. A limited number of the lightweight Stewart tanks and Amtracs were pressed into service, but it was too little, too late. Most of the vehicles never made it onto dry land but were left smoldering on the coral reef from the highly accurate rounds of enemy mortars or their big guns.

"Hey, Jock, over here!" Jock looked to his right to notice Owen waving with both hands. He acknowledges Owen's wave with a head nod almost losing his helmet in the process as he continued to move up on the beach out of the line of fire hoping that Owen does the same.

Jock's unit recollects itself and assesses their operational capability. Two of theirs are dead, the unit commander, and their corporal. They effectively had no one in charge. With this news, the highest-ranking soldier, being a private first class, went out to seek the nearest officer he could find. Within a few minutes he came back with a Staff Sergeant. "Sergeant Shields, are we glad to see you!" Shields surveyed the group closely. "Donahoe, you made it! It's about time you guys joined the party!"

Just fifty-four hours from the initial landings, Lt. Col. Kenneth McLeod issued orders to Captain Faraday to take I company of the 3/6 and execute passage of lines through the 1st battalion. Once performed, they would cross the airstrip and take a circuitous route to and along the northern side of the island and head due east to link up with Company K of the 2nd battalion, 8th Marines. Their mission was to seek out and silence any positions the enemy may have re-infiltrated back during the night. Upon completing this task, I Company was to pass through K Company to secure inland portions of the island so that mop-up operations could be conducted by the 27th Army infantry. The word was passed down to Second Lieutenant Bates and to Sergeant Shields that I Company would take the lead. Reports came back that there was still an enemy strongpoint just 300 yards east of the airstrip. They just didn't know their strength. Another unknown were snipers. Since the island was relatively barren of trees in part due to naval bombardment, there were still some areas just east of the airstrip where snipers could hide in the canopy and pick off the oncoming Marines. Their main concern were Japs burying themselves under their own dead waiting to be passed by, then come out in a banzai attack or worse, take a shot at their backs and then remain motionless and undetected under their protection.

Jock's unit was now collected behind a seawall made of logs. Their replacement unit commander started to speak. "As it is rather evident by now, the Japanese forces will fight to the last man at their positions and under no circumstance be taken as a prisoner of war. Therefore, we can anticipate fierce resistance to the bitter end. Any questions?" Sergeant Shields speaks first. "Yes sir, do we have any intel as to the enemy's strength in numbers and armor?" McLeod looks grimly at Shields before he responds. "We know there are perhaps three to five hundred or so of the enemy still dug in. Their armament consists of heavy machine guns, mortars, and we believe a few shore guns still are in operation. We also anticipate they will counterattack at night, so don't get too comfortable in your foxhole. They are fanatical." The entire company listened to McLeod's words very carefully. He then moved off with his radio man and small contingent of personnel to brief the other units on their situation. "You heard the man, now let's check your weapons and supplies before moving inland."

No unnecessary chances were going to be taken. I Company began their short trek up off the beach towards the defoliated trees where they would regroup before attempting to cross the open tarmac towards Beach Red 1 on the north side of the island.

To their surprise no direct contact with the enemy was encountered upon reaching the airstrip. There was the occasional mortar round of sporadic gun fire but no concentrated attempt to stop the Marines. It was almost eerie. Some of them were thinking a trap lay in store. It was 1330 hours when I Company reached their rally point on the northern side of the airstrip, which was only about 200 yards inland from Beach Red 1. After twenty minutes of reconnoitering, I Company changed direction and began their trek easterly. No sooner had they kick off their 2nd leg of their mission when mortar rounds started landing on their previous position decimating the remaining sparse vegetation. A close call for sure.

The air was still thick with smoke and visibility was poor. Faraday had Bates and Shields split the company into three squads. The lead squad would proceed down the middle with the trailing squads flanking each side. They were just 200 yards from linking up with K Company of the 2nd Battalion, 8th Marines.

Even with the haze, Jock could make out the two figures to his right and left with his peripheral vision. They were moving at the same steady pace, being careful not to make any more noise other than their boots setting down on a mixture of fallen debris from the jungle and sand. Before Jock heard the crackling noise of the Jap machine gun, the guy to his left went down to his knees and then fell backward. Chaos ensued from that moment on. Jock heard the screaming and yelling of Marines to hit the dirt and return fire, but in what direction? He did not see where the shooting was coming from. It didn't matter though because the entire company was returning fire into the thick pall in front of them. Just then, Jock caught a glimpse of a bright yellow flash up in a small cluster of the trees that remained intact almost directly above him. He aimed carefully and let out a three burst of projectiles at the shadowy figure. The figure stayed motionless for what seemed like eternity, and then pointed his weapon down at Jock. Before the sniper got off a return volley, a soldier with a BAR let loose a barrage of 7.62 lead jackets. The sniper's weapon fell to the ground first, with the sniper following suit an instant later.

Jock got up off the ground keeping his rifle on the fallen enemy as the man with the BAR walked over to him. Turning around to express his gratitude to the soldier that just saved his life, he realized it just wasn't any soldier. It was a former rival acquaintance of his when he played high school hockey. His name was Karl Bouldoukian from Southie. Everybody called him Duke. They had met when playing against each other all four years, and somehow, they became friends from afar. Probably because their lines were always pitted against each other. "Duke!"

"How the—"

"Small world, ain't it, pal? My unit got decimated trying to cross the coral reef at Beach Red 1 on D-Day, so I got thrown in with the Army's 27th Infantry Division as a Recon Unit."

Sergeant Shields went up to the Jap lying on the ground to make sure he was really a corpse, as the other Marines kept their arms at the ready for any other surprises. A corpsman rushed over to the fallen Marine that was just six feet away from Jock, but it was too late to do anything for him. Jock noticed that the dead Marine was riddled with bullet holes and his face was not distinguishable anymore. For all he knew, it might have been the guy standing next to him in the LVT with rosary beads in his hands murmuring a Hail Mary. He dropped to both knees and started to puke. After a minute, both Shields and Bouldoukian helped him up. "I'm sure glad you were there my ole friend."

"Yeah... me too," said Duke, handing Jock his rifle.

Vinnie examined the machine gun that the Jap had up in the tree. "How the hell did he get that thing up there with him and all this ammo?" Sergeant Shields rubbed his chin pondering Vinnie's question. "My guess is that he had help. He probably climbed the tree with a rope, then dropped one end down to have one of his buddies tie the gun so he could pull it up. Then they repeated this operation with the ammo. That means one thing... there's more Japs out there."

The Army captain ordered both his company and the Marine company to move forward taking special attention to the trees. Duke decided to stay alongside Jock to make sure he'd recovered from his initial engagement. Shields and Vinnie remained on the opposite side of Jock. Just ahead of them is a dense patch of overgrowth. Immediately, Shields recognized it as a potential pillbox or fortification and yelled out to his troops to drop. As the words are still reverberating from his mouth, the clump of logs and leaves lights up in a brilliant flash. The Marines hit the dirt for the second time this morning. Mere inches from Shield's position, the ground erupts with the spray of sand and splinters of wood. Two of the leathernecks fall backward like they are hit by an invisible freight train. The other Marines drop to their bellies and cover up as best as they can. Pinned down and protected by only how deep they were able to sink into the sand and volcanic ash, they were like the proverbial sitting duck just waiting to get picked off as soon as the Jap behind the machine gun detects any movement.

Second Lieutenant Bates reached out his hand to his radioman in a gesture to take the radio, only he was not greeted with any object. Bates looked around the best he could without gathering attention and sees his radioman, his head a bloody pulp. Bates sees that Jock has wormed his way over to the dead radioman and is able to remove the backpack from the lifeless body. He drags it over to Bates.

"Good work, Marine." Bates tries the radio only to find out it is dead also.

"Must have taken a round, Lieutenant," said Jock.

"Yeah, well ain't this our lucky day," said Bates as he throws the radio aside. The men knew that even if they could have gotten through to call up a flamethrower, it would not have mattered because none made it with the first wave and the few that made it in the second wave were in high demand on other parts of the island. They would have to come up with another idea.

Vinnie was nearest to a fallen tree, so he motioned to Shields. Shields picked up on Vinnie's gestures and started firing his weapon to give Vinnie a brief second or two to dash for the log. It worked, although Shields took a grazing round off his helmet. This gave Vinnie some limited space to throw out a grenade without exposing anything more than his throwing arm. Peering quickly over the log to assess the distance, he reached down to his ammo belt, grabbed a grenade, and pulled the pin while holding the clasp secure. The first lob fell way too short, and the grenade kicked up a plume of sand. The sergeant saw how far off the throw was and yelled out to Vinnie to throw another one 20 feet further. Again, the grenade exploded short of the intended destination, but Shields made use of the time that the enemy flinched from the near explosion and charged forward to flank the enemy's fortified position. The risk is that he didn't know if there were any other Japs in concealed positions. Within five seconds he found out as a barrage of lead flew by his head. Shields dove to the ground, but before he reached the acidic soil he felt a white-hot burning sensation across the top of his right shoulder. Knowing that he is hit, he doesn't call out. Instead, he reached for one of his own grenades and pulled the pin with his teeth. With all his might he threw the grenade, and it sailed right through the narrow opening for the gun placement. With a dull thud, smoke began to emanate from the fortification. There is silence. Shields peered out over the slight depression he is in and notices the fortification is still intact. "Damn! It must have been a dud." The blood has now saturated the sleeve to his shirt and the shock from the loss of blood starts to set in. The adrenaline from his actions starts to wear off and pain takes its place. The numbness in his fingers reaches all the way up his arm as well. The medic can't reach him without exposing himself to the submachine gun fire so Shields uses his hand to try to stem the flow of blood until help can arrive. He gets a little light-headed but is still coherent and hears some sort of armored track vehicle approaching. It's a Stuart Tank and it starts to shoot out a stream of flame into the pillbox incinerating everything and everyone inside. As for the other Japs flanking the pillbox, the Army infantry is able to out-flank their positions and commence sending them to meet their maker.

Jock and Vinnie reached Sergeant Shields just as he is coming in and out of consciousness from the loss of blood and the morphine administered by the medic. "DiNapoli, Donahoe! Get your—" He slips into unconsciousness again.

By nightfall I Company had lost eight Marines and six more are wounded, including Sergeant Shields. Vinnie, Chaz, Owen, Duke, and Jock came away unscathed, but night was rapidly approaching, and they knew it wasn't over.

A replacement company from the 27th Army infantry division moves through I Company and takes a flanking position along their northern perimeter. Duke says his goodbyes to Jock and the others and Jock responds by saying "See you on the ice down on Chandlers Pond my friend." With a nod Duke mingles in with the rest of the 27th and disappears. This gives Jock and his buddies a chance to eat and reflect on the events of the day.

At about 2100 hours, Second Lieutenant Bates came by the fox-holes where Jock and his buddies are dug in. Hey, LT, how's the Sarge doing?" He's doing better than we thought. It turns out that he lost a lot of blood, but the wound missed all vital organs and bone. In fact, he's requested that he remain with the unit. We should be able to see him tomorrow."

"That's swell; I don't think the Japs stand a chance now." Bates moved on to check on his other Marines.

Within a minute after Second Lieutenant Bates left, a loud shriek spooked every Marine within listening distance. Each Ma-rine stopped whatever they were doing and readied themselves for the inevitable. They would not have to wait very long.

A few minutes later there was a loud shriek from deep inside the jungle. At least 50 Japanese imperial soldiers, better known as the Rigosentai, started screaming Banzai and charged directly at I Company and the company from the 27th Army infantry. I Compa-ny's back-up radioman frantically called in for artillery fire just 50 yards in front of their position, but this did not deter the obsessed enemy. They kept coming. Jock's platoon opened fire first, then the other platoons followed suit. Still, some of the enemy make it to the Marines' front lines, and a viscous onslaught in hand-to-hand combat takes place. The sound of men screaming from being slashed by a samurai sword or being bayoneted in the abdomen could not be ignored. Anxiety was at fever pitch. The adrenaline in each Marine was running like a raging bull in their veins. A Jap reached Jock's foxhole and jabbed his fixed bayonet at him. Jock averted the thrust and pulled the trigger on his carbine. One of the three rounds hit his assailant in the shoulder, but the Jap took a second lunge at Jock missing his face by less than an inch. Jock reached up, grabbed the rifle with one hand, and using his other hand took out his hunters' knife from his sheath and plunged it deep into the Jap's thigh. The Rigosentai writhed in pain and fell to his knees. Jock withdrew the knife and plunged it into him again, but this time right into his heart. With eyes bulging out of his sockets he stared directly into Jock's eyes in utter disbelief, blood now oozing out of his mouth and the open wound in his chest. He fell forward right onto Jock.

The shooting and screaming brings Jock back to the ensuing battle. He pushes the dead Jap off him and looks around to see if anymore were coming his way. It is almost pitch black due to the 1/8th moon and the thick smoke from burning vehicles and pillboxes. He cannot make out if the figures that are standing around him are his own or the enemy. Since the figures are standing low and still, he assesses they are US Marines. Then a familiar voice reaches his ears. "I Company, regroup."

Second Lieutenant Bates is standing about fifteen feet from Jock's foxhole with about six other Marines around him. "I want DiNapoli and Donahoe to recon for any wounded Marines that need medical assistance. Friberg, and Brady, make sure you provide cover and make sure there are no Japs playing possum. Stick 'em to make sure. Villanova and Andrews, cover their six. The rest of the unit keep your eyes and ears open. You see anything coming from that direction, shoot first and ask questions later."

Jock and Vinnie slowly and methodically probe the area for any wounded buddies. Vinnie keeps watch for any movement to their front while Jock conducts a peripheral recon.

"Hey, it's Malloy. He's dead. Looks like he took two of the bastards with him." Second Lieutenant Bates came up to where the fallen Marine was. He notices that the dead Marine's knife is still clenched in his hands, but there is a bayonet in his back. The medic confirms that Malloy is dead, and with help from some other Marines places the body on a litter and takes it to the rear of the unit. For the rest of the night, no one dared to close their eyes.

All tallied, I Company lost five more men and four wounded or out of action. The Army unit's losses were greater; nine dead, six wounded including their unit commander. By morning, the US forces counted forty-two Japanese dead. They suspect that a few have slipped back into the bush. It was a bitter engagement. No one suspected the Japs to come at them head on like that, armed only with their rifles, bayonets, and a few with swords. The Marines were able to pick off half of them before they reached their lines.

A lull in the combat has given the men a chance to rest and re-supply their ammo. Second Lieutenant Bates receives orders to continue easterly to reinforce the lead elements of 2/8. At 0900 they move to reach their final destination. Chaz and Jock take the lead. Just 30 yards ahead lay a cluster of logs arranged in a pattern that would be perfect for a sniper to be completely concealed. Jock signals Chaz by raising his right hand and motions Chaz to circle to the right. Jock circles around to the left. The rest of the squad holds up until they get the clear signal. Suddenly, there is a flash from the log pile. Both Jock and Chaz hit the ground firing their M1 carbines into the sniper's nest, but the logs protect the shooter. Chaz reaches for a grenade, yells out to Jock, and lobs it into the center of the pile. Wood splinters the size of combat knives shoot out in every direction. There is an eerie silence for a moment.

Figuring the enemy is blown to bits, Chaz worms his way nearer. Jock notices the business end of a rifle protruding through two logs and yells to Chaz to take cover as he empties his clip in the spot where the enemy rifle was. The steel cylinder of the enemy rifle is aiming up to the sky. Chaz slowly gets up and makes his way to the logs. He sees two dead Rigosentai: one of them with only the remnants of a torso from the grenade, the other with a gaping bullet hole through the forehead. "Good shooting Donahoe!"

Jock gets up and approaches the bullet riddled log stronghold. He notices that the Jap he shot was just a kid, no more than 15 or so.

His eyes are still wide open as if he wasn't supposed to die. The rest of the platoon walked by without saying a word. It is only 09:30 but they are already beat from their two engagements.

On the evening of D-Day plus 3, mop-up operations are winding down. All toll, the enemy lost over four thousand strong while the US forces suffered nearly three thousand casualties. The battle has been fought and won. The island belongs to the 2nd Marine Division and the 27th Army Infantry.

Chapter XIII

Taking Solace

Three days after the island is secured, the Marines of the 3/6 and the 2/8 returned to their troopships. With Tarawa wrested away from the Japanese empire, the weary contingent of Task Force 53 set sail back to New Zealand for some well-earned R and R.

Once on-board, Chaz and Vinnie were able to track down the whereabouts and condition of Sergeant Shields. As luck would have it, Shields was returned to the Harris because his wounds weren't critical, and the troopship had some capability to treat non-life-threatening wounds.

Sergeant Shields hears muffled voices and opens his eyes. He thought he was having a nightmare but then realized the four familiar voices he heard were on both sides of his gurney.

"Hey, Sarge. How's that million-dollar wound?" Shields was getting mighty antsy being cooped up in a bed for the last four days and his response was to the point. "Look, you prima-donnas. When I get out of here, I'm gonna let you get acquainted with the toe of my boon dockers!"

"Aw, Sergeant. Is that any way to treat the guys that saved your life?" chided Owen. Vinnie, Jock and Chaz took turns at smacking Owen in the back of his head. Owen took it all in good fun. He was simply happy he and his gang made it out all in one piece.

Jock placed his hand on the sergeant's shoulder. "Welcome back Sergeant. We were worried about you for a while."

"Ya, Sarge. We thought we were never going to hear that warm friendly voice of yours again," chirped Owen. Vinnie and Chaz tried to hide their smirks knowing that Shields would chastise them if they contributed to the banter. Propping himself up as best he could with one arm in a sling, a small grin grew on his face. "You boys did good; real good. I can now call you Marines." Chaz leaned in closer. "The doc says you will be back with the unit by the time we reach Wellington. The bullet went right through your shoulder and missed all the vitals. Some bone fragments, but that's the worst of it. It tore a big hole, and you lost a lot of blood, but they say you are one tough SOB." Shields settled back in a less upright position. "Well, you don't think I was gonna buy the farm knowing you four pretty boys would relish in not receiving another ass chewing do ya?"

The four of them laughed. "Good to see you haven't lost that charming personality," replied Vinnie as he pulled out of his pocket a small canteen of torpedo juice. "Here, take a swig of this. It's our victory toast for surviving our first baptismal of fire." Vinnie extended the container to Shields first. "What's in it DiNapoli?"

"Oh, just a little concoction I brewed up back in Hawaii. It's a mix of grain alcohol and pineapple juice."

The medic came over and told the Marines they must leave. Shields took another swig of the extract and wiped his mouth with his good arm. "You did good out there. You are now battle-hardened Marines. The kind of Marines I want with me when we storm through the Gates of Hell."

"Semper-Fi" came out of the group in unison.

The 3/6 would not stay around Betio for very long. Their new orders were to go back to New Zealand for some rest and some additional training in the jagged foothills around Camp McKay.

On their voyage back to New Zealand, the guys were able to make frequent visits with their Sergeant in the infirmary to the point that it was starting to irritate him to no end. Maybe it was just the morphine but the sarge seemed a bit out of sorts. Vinnie, Chaz, Owen, and Jock couldn't remember a time when Shields was so distant. Something serious must have happened thought the foursome.

The good news was that their Sergeant would be getting out of the infirmary before arriving into port at Wellington.

As the USS Harris was entering the harbor at Wellington, Jock noticed Shields by himself puffing on a Lucky Strike, so he joined him. "What's troubling you, Sergeant?"

Shields took a long draw on the cigarette. "I just found out my best friend was killed in action on the Solomon Islands back in August."

Jock didn't know what to say. "I'm sorry, Sarge."

The sergeant just stared out in the opposite direction towards where all the buzz in the harbor was going on. "We grew up together, played sports together, and got drunk together. Up until we enlisted. He wanted Army; I chose Marine Corps."

"He must have been a helluva soldier, Sarge."

There was another pause from Shields. "He was a helluva friend." With that, Jock knew enough to leave the sergeant alone to let him grieve without any more interruptions.

On December 3rd, 1943, back at Camp McKay, elements of the 2nd Marine Division were being reorganized, re-supplied, and re-energized with fresh replacements mixed in with their battle-hardened brethren. Sergeant Shields, fully recovered from his earlier wounds, walked into the hut where his platoon was relaxing. The men seemed anxious to get back into the thick of things, even after what they experienced on Tarawa. Shields was not as eager. He felt they needed some time to lick their wounds.

"Marines, assemble out in the yard in fifteen minutes and have all your gear with you. We are going on a little hike!" roared the sergeant.

Sergeant Shields was back to active combat status, and all was well with I Company. Jock and Vinnie were being trained to use flame throwers, although the pack was a bit too cumbersome for Jock to handle for a long duration. The apparatus weighed almost as much as he did. During one training occasion, Jock had to climb down a rock-strewn valley only to repeatedly hit the bottom of the steel tank filled with a gelatin-like gasoline mix on the rocks. By the time he made it down to the bottom, the fuel had leaked out leaving the tank almost empty. It was a surprise to everyone that the concoction did not ignite from the sparks created when the steel tank impacted the rocks. All the guys wanted the Saint Christopher pin that Jock had attached to his flapped pocket of his khakis. It brought memories of Monica back to him; wondering if he would ever see or hear from her again. Although he only knew her for a short time back at Camp Elliot, he just could not get her out of his head. He was troubled that he had such deep affections for two women.

Vinnie climbed back up to the pile of rocks that Jock was resting on. "Whadaya say we jury-rig some padding on the bottom of those tanks so the next time that happens you don't become toast?"

"Not a bad idea Vin. I think I'm pushing my luck a bit." Jock hoisted the empty tanks back on his back and proceeded to walk down the remaining leg of the hill to catch up with the rest of the platoon. Shields was standing along the side of the road as the Marines took five before continuing the rest of their ten-mile exercise. "Donahoe, I want you to relinquish the thrower to Owen P. Chester the 3rd and take the scout position with Azuroni."

"Okay Sarge. Sorry about the tanks to the flame thrower. I had no idea I cracked them open."

"We're just lucky you didn't fry yourself and half the squad Donahoe. Now get going and grab Chester's rifle." Jock was already in motion before Shields had finished.

As soon as Jock was out of hearing, Vinnie walked up to Shields. "Hey Sarge, the darn tanks on the flame thrower are just too big for Donahoe."

"I know, I know, DiNapoli. I'll find a replacement tomorrow."

Back in Camp McKay, after their 3-day exercise in the outback, the Marines of the 6th Regiment had a few days of rest and relaxation which gave them time to start missing home again.

It's been over a year since Jock and most of his comrades had seen their families and loved ones. It was taking its toll on Jock. He was surprised that he missed his dad so much. For most of his childhood, Dad was away in Washington, DC as a legal counsel representative on government contracts. His occasional surrogate parents were Aunt Mary, Uncle Tom, and Aunt Lil, as well as his cousin Rose Murphy. They were the ones that looked after the children while Dad was away. Jock still held onto a small photo of his mom, but he could hardly remember her. Still, he would try to imagine what it would have been like to have grown up with a doting mother and disciplinarian father. His thoughts turned to his brother Bob who was in Louisiana for his military training before being shipped out to parts unknown, but likely overseas to fight the Nazis. He pulled out the last letter he received from his brother.

Hi, Brother. Hope this letter finds you in the best of health and things are going in your favor. Most of all, did you hear where the Marines just landed on Tarawa and the fighting is tough going? I take it that your outfit may be one of those in the mix, so I am crossing my fingers and praying for your safety. Well, no easy way to say this but I just arrived at Camp Polk, Louisiana for basic training with the Army. Soon I will be in tip top shape and ready for anything that comes my way. Dad is still down in Washington, DC and sis still at Regis. They are both doing well and wanted me to tell you that they miss you. Did you hear that the Red Sox came in second place this year? They were only three and one-half games out of first place but lost four in a row. They should have a great team next year. Hopefully, we will be able to go see them next year. Please write when you get a chance, so we know you are okay.

Take care of yourself

Your Little Brother but Better Hockey Player

Jock's thoughts turned back to his sister Evelyn and his girl Jeanne back in Brighton. His daydream was broken when Vinnie, Chaz, and Owen came crashing into the Quonset hut laughing and cajoling each other over some prank they successfully executed at the mess tent. It seemed that someone mailed Vinnie a rubber chicken as a gag, so Vinnie wanted to make good use of the almost real-life bird and drop it in the stew pot. From about 50 feet away, they watched as one of the cooks noticed something floating in the pot. He took a pair of wooden utensils and carefully lifted the fowl up out of the pot. He looked around to make sure no one was looking and placed it back in the pot and walked away. The guys almost pissed their pants trying to hold their laughter.

The 3/6 got word they were going back to Hawaii before the end of the month for some R and R and for additional training. The thing was, nobody knew what type of training they were going to receive and for what purpose. No letters could be sent out until they reached their destination. After boarding the troopship and settling in, they learned that their next destination would be back to Pearl Harbor.

Christmas of 1943 was spent on board the USS Wharton. Other troopships in the convoy that were making the trip were the USS Harris and the Zeilin. Everybody was looking forward to being back on US soil.

Little information was given about any progress being made against the Japanese. They would just have to wait until they got back on dry land.

On January 2, 1944, segments of the convoy separated as they neared Hawaii. Some went directly to Pearl. The Wharton headed to the Big Island of Hawaii.

Seeing Hawaii's tallest summit, Mauna Kea from about 7 miles offshore on the USS Wharton brought an uproar from the troops that must have been heard on the mainland. Everybody was scrambling to get topside to see the top of the mountain covered with snow. Many of the men could not believe this island paradise could ever have snow. Luckily, by the time Jock and the guys got topside they could see the magnificent mountainous terrain and beautiful vegetation on the lower elevations as well. They were now only about three miles from land. Jock, Vin, and Chaz stuck close together disembarking the troop ship in Hilo. Owen and Sergeant Shields were nowhere to be found.

Fortunately, the entire contingent of Marines was headed to the same destination point on the Big Island. Once the Marines disembarked, they were loaded onto trucks and transported several miles to Camp Tarawa at Kamuela situated near vast sprawling lava fields. The terrain was craggy and jagged, resulting in numerous mishaps during their stay. "So, this is paradise," Jock thought to himself.

The following morning, Sergeant Shields found them, but Owen seemed to be MIA. "Hey Sarge, it's good to see you. What did you do with Owen?" The sergeant informed them that Owen came down with Malaria, so he had to be quarantined from the rest of the troops. "He is hurting really bad. The Docs don't know if he is going to make it." The guys remained silent as they were directed to a makeshift amphitheater partially carved out of the jungle and former lava pools created from extinct volcano eruptions.

There was a slight cool breeze coming out of the northwest, but the Marines in Jock's platoon were still sweating due to the high humidity.

Some high-level brass were on the wooden stage-like platform waiting for all the men to file in. Within fifteen minutes, all was quiet.

The man with the most ribbons, pins, and stars on his uniform walked up to the podium. "Marines, I am Lieutenant General Holland Smith. I am Ground Commanding General of the Expeditionary Troops, Northern Troops, and Landing Force of the 2nd Marine

Division. I want to take this opportunity to say how proud the United States Marine Corps, the Joint Chiefs of Staff, and the President of the United States are of your heroic efforts in this war. You have proven there is no other military organization in the world that is tougher than you are. Your bravery is second to none.

Many of you have lost friends, comrades, and even loved ones since this war began. Much blood has been spilled. We did not start this war, but by God we are going to end it. You are here today because we are calling upon you once again. Our next objective is to defeat the enemy on the Islands of the Marianas, specifically Saipan, Tinian, and Guam. It will be called Operation Forager and we are designated as Task Force 56. Starting today, you will be receiving additional amphibious training. Your rest is over. The time to bring this war to a close is now."

After the announcement, the men were led to the canteen tents for breakfast. It was only 07:00 and it was going to be a long, long day.

Jock, Vinnie, and Chaz grabbed a bench to chow down their green ham and eggs. Shields sat with the other sergeants from the other platoons.

"Hey Jock, what do you think we are up to?" queried Chaz. "I think we are going to get a little wet my friend." They chuckled and finished their breakfast.

For the next few months, an extensive training program was implemented giving the Marines advanced readiness prior to the invasion of the Mariana Islands. Emphasis was placed on individual and small unit training. These exercises were conducted both day and night in terrain varying from jungle to volcanic sediment.

During the period of March 12th through the 31st, the Marines of the 6th Marine Regiment conducted amphibious maneuvers on the beaches of Maalaea Bay on Maui. Jock and his platoon performed their tasks without any mishaps. The weather was calm and clear. It wasn't the same for the members of the 2nd Battalion, 8th Marines. On May 14th during their last rehearsal, three operational accidents occurred which resulted with several Marines losing their lives. The amphibious landing craft tanks (LCTs) full of Marines inside were secured to the decks of three LSTs when the weather turned. The waves battered the LSTs with the force of a freight train pitching the ships violently till the cables that were securing the LCTs snapped pitching some of the amphibious craft overboard. Several men did not make it out of the submerged LCTs.

Although a tragedy, the rehearsals proved to be invaluable for the ship to shore movement of troops and equipment as well as making modifications to their communication network.

The Marines moved on and conducted their final full-scale Corps (2nd and 4th Marine divisions) landing at Maalaea Bay, Maui on May 17 through May 19, 1944. Fortunately, that rehearsal went off without any incidents. All the Marines had to do now is wait for their orders to embark for somewhere in the central pacific.

Due to the enormous size of the task force and the complexity of the logistics, the embarkation phase needed to be split up at two locations. One contingent would assemble in Pearl Harbor and the other in Maalaea Bay on May 21st.

Unfortunately, disaster struck again for the portion of the task force at Pearl Harbor. Ammunition being loaded on to a LST exploded resulting in the destruction of six LSTs. Worse yet, the 2nd Marine Division lost 95 men and the 4th Division lost 112 men. Jock's regiment was fortunately part of the contingent embarking from Maalaea Bay, but that did not seem to matter much to the boys of the 3/6. They knew some of those Marines that perished.

After days of sorting out the melee and mishaps of that tragic event, the operation was ready to proceed. The LSTs loaded with assault troops and their equipment were given the designation as the Northern Attack Force commanded by Lieutenant General Holland M. Smith The armada left their safe harbors in the Hawaiian Islands on May 29, 1944. Their destination would be Saipan, some 3500 miles away.

Chapter XIV

The Beginning of the End

Finally, after months of additional training and R&R, Jock was ready to see action again. He, along with the rest of the Marines knew deep down those bullets flying are indiscriminate and will hit whatever object is in its path. The feeling of invincibility was lost after their first encounter with the enemy. But this is what soldiers do. This is what they're trained for. Jock knew everybody was feeling afraid. It is how you deal with that fear. Bravery, courage, valor, call it what you want. Jock was prepared to do whatever was necessary to accomplish their mission; along with every other Marine headed back into harm's way.

All letters to their loved ones were written while still in Hawaii. Jock was thinking about his dad, and this is the letter he wrote to him.

Dear Dad,

I can't tell you where we are or going but I can tell you that I am with the best fellas the Marine Corps has ever produced.

Don't worry about me because I am feeling fine and getting along swell. I would have written sooner but I have been kept rather busy. We have gotten very good, and I pity those Japs when this group gets a hold of them. Dad, will you send me a hunting knife and a flashlight. I need these two articles awfully bad. I also need some air mail stamps so the letters I send you arrive sooner.

I'm sitting here with all the fellas talking about whose house they are going to visit on our way home after the war. Some of the fellas are from Boston and vicinity. There's Ronnie Andrews and David Villanova (we call him Dee) from Weymouth They were friends before enlisting and two of the toughest Marines I have ever met. And of course, not to mention my other pals, Vinnie, Chaz, Owen, and Sergeant Roger Shields from Braintree.

Well Dad, I guess I have said enough for now. Tell all the cousins and everyone I was asking for them and that I miss them all.

God bless and Not to Worry.
Your Loving Son
Jock
P.V.C. John W. Donahoe, USMCR

The LST was loaded with Marines, their quarters were cramped so to kill as much time as they could until they were called into action most entertained themselves with card games, chess, or craps. In Jock's case it was the latter.

Playing craps with fifteen other Marines in the bowels of a naval troopship wasn't Jock's idea of preparing for their next amphibious assault. But there wasn't much else to do. They were still a few days away from reaching their next destination and seeing action. But this time Jock was up one hundred and twenty bucks, and it was his turn to throw the dice. Big Eddy McFee had not won a game since boarding the ship in Hawaii. He was not about to let two months' pay just slip away.

It was quite a surprise when Jock bumped into Big Eddy as they were boarding the troop transport ship in Maui. It was almost a comedy of errors. Some 'wet behind the ears' Marine replacement dropped his sack while walking up the gantry and it rolled right into Big Eddy's path as he was looking to one side taking in the size of the ship.

He sensed an oncoming hazard approaching, he tried to avert it by stepping over it, but it was just too big. The bag almost knocked big Eddy down. No matter though because the damage was done. As soon as Big Eddy shifted his momentum, the guy behind him was unaware and the next guy behind him got caught up in the commotion. Soon there were guys bumping and falling over each other just like dominoes. That's when Big Eddy noticed Jock. He was about ten guys behind when Eddy hollered out: "Jocko! It's Eddy!"

Jock looked up from the commotion and found Eddy immediately. How could he miss a big red-headed Irishman with the broadest shoulders of anybody he ever knew?

"Eddy! How the hell.... what the hell are you doing here?" Eddy made it down the plank bumping into every leatherneck on the way. Some of them none too happy but that did not bother Eddy. He was about to catch up with his best pal from Brighton. What were the odds of that?

Eddy wrapped his big arms around Jock lifting him right up off the narrow gangway. "Jeezuz Eddy, you're squeezing the crap out of me." Eddy put him down. "It's great to see you too pal." There now was a huge gap from where Eddy and Jock were and the guys ahead of them on the gangway. Some of the Marines behind the two were now grumbling to them to get moving. "Pipe down" retorted Eddy picking up his duffel and proceeding on up the gangway trying to talk with Jock in the procession.

At the top of the gangway Eddy and Jock were directed to their Battalion's quarters. "Look it buddy, I'll catch up with you later tonight. Maybe we can get some action going in a craps game."

"Swell, Eddy, sounds like a pretty good plan to me." They parted ways until later that evening.

Jock could not help but remember the last time he had seen Eddy. It was at the Marine Recruitment Center in Allston, May 16, 1942. It was only a year and a half ago, but it seemed like a century. Both grew up in Brighton, Massachusetts, attended the same parochial grade school, and then on to high school. They became close friends in the 7th grade when Eddy, at least 50 pounds heavier and several inches taller than Jock, ran into trouble with some local neighborhood punks. This older group of three decided to block Eddy's passage through an alley on his way home from school just to see what Eddy would do. As he tried to pass around the three thugs, one of them stuck out his leg and tripped him. Eddy sprung up off the cobblestones and tackled the offender. Though they were two years older, Eddy was as big and strong as any of them. When seeing that their buddy was getting the worst of it, the other two decided to join in the fracas by kicking Eddy in the head and ribs. While the beating continued, Jock appeared out of nowhere and grabbed the nearest one with both hands and flung him against the brick wall. The second punk turned to respond but Jocko was too quick, his right foot found his mark and the punk keeled over in agony. The third and final offender was still trying to finish off Big Eddy but to no avail. Eddy, having noticed Jock coming to his rescue, gained a second wave of adrenaline. With both arms, Eddy picked the remaining dirtball right off the ground and threw him into a collection of overfilled garbage cans. Eddy and Jock looked at their handiwork and decided now might be a good time to leave before the punks were able to regroup or others might appear.

Eddy remained loyal to Jock ever since. Those punks never gave either of them a second glance ever again.

Still, the thought of Eddy losing more money to Jock wasn't very appealing, so he decided to take things into his own hands. Just when he was about to let the dice fly, Eddy grabbed his arm firmly preventing the dice from meeting their destiny. Jock looked up in disbelief. "What the hell are you doing? I'm on a roll!"

"Not with my money," Eddie blurted. "I think the dice are loaded."

That's all it took. With the pent-up frustration of being on board a ship loaded down with two thousand Marines for days was like lighting a match to a powder keg. Jock crouched down low and lunged at Eddy lifting him up off the deck with his right shoulder. They came crashing down together with Jock on top. However, it didn't take long for Big Eddy's size and strength to reverse the situation.

Some of the other Marines did not know what to make of the brawl. They looked on in disbelief until a grin as wide as Jock could muster gave away their little performance. Just then the alarms clanged... battle stations!

Unbeknownst to the troops, the Task Force had joined up with other portions of the invasion fleet somewhere north of the Solomon Islands. Combined, the naval armada consisted of over 600 ships of every shape and size. They still had several hundred miles to go to reach their staging area on the island of Eniwetok, but discovery of their flotilla was inevitable. Action was coming their way.

A Japanese reconnaissance plane was spotted flying a routine patrol out from Guam and stumbled upon the US Invasion Fleet. It was shot down, but it wasn't long after that three Japanese Zeros came into view and made a beeline towards the fleet.

The three Zeros swooped down on the task force below, American F6F-3 Hellcat fighters climbed to engage them head on. Lieutenant Mickey Bowen flying in lead formation squeezed off what seemed to be an endless trail of 75- millimeter steel-jacketed rounds. The first Zero burst into a thousand pieces of flaming shrapnel, which found its lethal trajectory to the Zero on his right wing. The third Zero dove past the American Fighters and headed straight for the nearest target it could find, the USS Bunker Hill. All guns were blazing away at the last Japanese plane, but its pilot was a kamikaze bent on bringing honor to the Emperor.

Just when it looked like the plane was going to hit the Bunker Hill amidships, the left wing fell off and the plane spiraled harmlessly into the ocean less than 100 yards away from its starboard side.

While all this was going on, Jock and Big Eddy shared a ringside view from the aft of their troop carrier. "Jesus, did you see that!" Eddy remarked.

"Yes, I think we were lucky this time. I just hope our luck holds out. Now let's go pick up my winnings from the mess hall deck."

To make matters worse, the last Japanese fighter pilot was able to send a frantic communiqué to his base providing notice that the Americans are coming. This started a whole series of events within the Japanese Imperial Navy that would shape the future events known as The Battle of the Philippine Sea or yet better known as The Great Marianas Turkey Shoot. Once things settled back down, the Task Force continued to their objective, the invasion of Saipan.

Chapter XV

Follow Me

Look here my friends as you pass by.
As you are now, so once was I.
As I am now, soon you will be.
So, prepare for death…and follow me.

The operation was called Forager, which entailed the invasion of Saipan, Tinian, and Guam, all part of the Marianas in the Central Pacific. Tokyo laid 1250 miles away.

Following the success of the US armed forces "Leapfrog" strategy, which was to seize those islands essential to the war effort and bypass other strongly held intervening islands thereby isolating the enemy by cutting off their supplies in defense of those islands.

For the Japanese, Saipan was the strategic point in the defense of the Mariana Islands and their primary supply and communications center for the entire Central Pacific.

For the United States, Saipan and Tinian would be the stepping-stone in which their new B-29 bombers would be able to reach the Japanese mainland by air without having to refuel. It would be later known as the beginning of the end of the Japanese empire. It was here that the United States would launch the planes that would deliver the only two atomic bombs in history, Hiroshima and Nagasaki.

Saipan is the second largest of the Mariana Islands, 14 miles in length and about 6.5 miles at its widest point. Its topographical features consisted of rugged wooded mountains and ringed with coral reefs. That one feature would cause a significant challenge for the amphibious assault teams as it would squeeze the invasion force into tight quarters where the Japanese could focus all their firepower on. Basically, it was a death trap or more commonly called nowadays as a kill box for Marines and Army.

All the Marine units were briefed on their objectives and missions en route. The 6th Marines were to land on the Charan Kanoa beaches situated on the Southwesterly side of Saipan. Japanese defenses would be strongest there. There were four designations for the beaches, yellow, blue, green, and red. Each beach was to have three separate landing areas, the 3/6 were tasked to secure Beach Red 1, 2, and 3, the most northerly of all the beaches. Jock's LVT would attempt to land on Red 2.

On June 9th, Jock's troopship entered Eniwetok Lagoon for final assembly and staging. Jock and Vinnie gazed out from the starboard side of their troop transport and saw the largest gathering of ships anyone has ever seen or likely will ever see again. The men were in awe. There were aircraft carriers and battleships, cruisers, destroyers, and, of course, troop ships, lots and lots of troop ships. The Marines were packed like sardines on those troop ships. In total, it was estimated a combined force of 127,500 US military personnel on 600 ships would participate in the action.

On June 11th, the LSTs and transports of Task Force 56 carrying the assault forces left Eniwetok directly for Saipan, some 1000 miles away.

About this same time, intense preparatory bombardment from sea commenced some 10,000 yards offshore of Saipan by Task Force 58 commanded by Vice Admiral Marc A. Mitscher. The reason for this distance was twofold; fear of possible enemy land mines, and to be far enough away from the enemy's artillery and shore batteries entrenched on the islands. The bombing continued day and night for three and one half days.

In addition to the naval bombardment from Force 58's battle ships and cruisers, the carriers, some 200 miles east of the islands, conducted daytime sorties by air to gather intel on the effect of the bombardment and to strafe any enemy positions found on Saipan, Tinian, and Guam.

Unfortunately, the effectiveness of all this naval bombardment was limited as the Japanese were so well entrenched, and had excellent skills using camouflage that unless it was a direct hit their guns remained intact.

Jock and his platoon could hear the rumble of the big guns pounding the islands from a couple hundred miles away. It gave the

Marines some comfort knowing the enemy ranks may be thinned out... they hoped.

On the morning of June 14th, the LSTs has reached their line of departure some 5000 yards from the beach for the next day. Breakfast was being served. Jock got to find a spot on deck close to Sergeant Shields, Vinnie, Big Eddy, and Chaz.

"Ahhh," spoused Vinnie. "Scrambled eggs, fried potatoes, toast, and some piece of mystery meat which I can only assume is ham. What I can't figure out is what this green sheen of goop is."

"You don't want to know, DiNapoli. I advise you to eat it anyhow, it might help your shooting accuracy." The boys chuckled at Sergeant Shields suggestion. It was needed as anxiety was setting in on all aboard.

Sermon was given to all that wanted to participate on the late afternoon of the 14th. Jock, Big Eddy, Vinnie, and Sergeant Shields were catholic and welcomed the mass on deck. Chaz and Owen opted out. In the distance they could just make out the flickering of the battleships' big guns firing, and then the thunder that came seconds later.

Afterwards, the men were updated on their specific tasks as new intel was shared by their commanding officer of the 6th Marines.

Colonel James P. Riseley had a low, calm, monotonous voice when he spoke. "This is what to expect. We estimate the enemy is around 32,000 strong combined on the three islands with Saipan having about 19,000 of that. Our landing force will put almost 80,000 Marines and some 50,000 Army on these islands in a matter of a couple of days. You will not be alone. The enemy is well entrenched and will fight 'til their dying breath. So, keep your head down, move fast when the ramp drops down, and get to the beach as quickly as possible. As you already know we have been given the tasks to secure Beaches 1, 2, and 3 and then wait for the second wave to reinforce our positions before moving inland. Lieutenant Colonel John Easley will lead the 3/6. Lieutenant Colonel Raymond Murray has the 2/6, and I will go in with the 1/6. We have trained long and hard for this and expect all of you to do your job as I know you will. Semper Fi Marines and God Bless." The Marines returned the motto so the entire transport could hear. That put a grin on Jock's face.

"Here we go again," murmured Vinnie. Jock looked at Vinnie, then at the others. "Yup. Another day of sun and sand. What else could you ask for?" Each of his friends were able to force a slight grin on their faces. The Marines got very little sleep that night.

About 0400 hours on the morning of June 15th, the public address system on all the boats came alive. "All Hands... General Quarters." The Marines in the crowded quarters below the decks of the LSTs muster. Their breakfast would be the same as just about every other day on the LSTs, except the green ham was replaced with steak. Not many had much of an appetite as the ones that saw action on Tarawa and other islands knew what a bobbing and weaving on the Higgins boats and the other amphibious craft can do to one's stomach when its full.

Last minute checks were made such as making sure they all had extra ammunition, c-rations, canteens full of water, and the all-important shovel which would be needed.

At 05:42 hours, approximately 5000 yards from shore, the orders came down from senior command. "Land the landing force." Then, the Battalion Commander's yell out, "Lower All Boats." Jock was in one of the LVTs (an upgraded version of the Amtrac) along with Owen. Sergeant Shields, Vinnie, Chaz, and Big Eddy were in a different LVT.

The large bay doors on each LST opened and the ramps dropped into the water. Then the LVTs and other various amphibious craft entered the waters. In total, 719 crafts and the like motored under their own power to the line of departure some 1250 yards away from their LSTs and formed a counterclockwise running circle until all invasion craft were in position.

The line of departure was now some 4000 yards from the beaches as the Amtracs and Higgins boats continued to form before receiving the orders to head in.

Jock took out the knife he received from his dad. He didn't think it would get here on time as he lost his government issued k-knife on Tarawa. His mind raced with all the memories of home. He doesn't recall this happening when they stormed the beaches at Tarawa. This time felt different. He wished his other buddies, and the sergeant were with him in this Amtrac. Putting the knife back in its sleeve, he looked at his watch, 07:00 hours. The early morning haze had lifted, and the sun was shining bright. As far as the eye could see were ships and landing craft. Peering towards the island he could make out Mount Tapotchau to the south and the lower plateau-like Mount Marpi to the north.

Within minutes, the guns from the US fleet opened a crescendo of rapid firing from their battleships and destroyers. Then, almost as quickly as it started, it ceased, and waves of fighters and bombers went in to extoll their pound of flesh from the enemy positions. Once the planes were returning to the carriers, the big guns started pounding the island for the last time before the central control vessel hoisted its signal flag for H-Hour.

Just after 0800 hours the engines on all the Amtracs roared louder. Someone shouted, "This is it!" One by one the amphibian vehicles representing the first wave formed a V formation and raced toward the beaches. The remaining waves of the assault craft started their charge towards the beaches in intervals so as not to congest all the craft making for an easier target for the enemy. It would take about twenty-five minutes before they reached the reefs as they were still some 3500 yards out.

The boats were in full throttle thrashing about from the waves. Jock, as well as many others had to place a hand onto their helmets even though they were strapped under their chins. A smoke screen was laid down in front of them in the hopes it would obscure the enemy zeroing in on the craft.

As the LVTs reached the coral reefs, a withering barrage of mortar and artillery rounds exploded all around the LVTs. Some of the Higgins boats got bogged down on the reefs and manmade obstacles of logs and debris some 200 yards from the beach. Most of the Amtracs managed to get through.

Jock looked out to see flags which he remembered seeing when they stormed Tarawa. The flags were placed there by the Japanese as markers which enabled their artillery to specifically pinpoint their firepower on the assault wave of Marines. Then suddenly, there is this thundering explosion to Jock's right and a huge water geyser erupts where a LVT once was. It was gone, just like that. It must have been a direct hit. All that went through Jock's mind was if it was the Amtrac that Sergeant Shields, Vinnie, and Big Eddy were on. "Oh God, I hope not." He reached for the cross around his neck that Mr. Hurley gave him before going off to war. It brought a warm sensation and a calming aura to him. Then, another thunderous explosion and a brilliant white light.

Tell Dad not to worry
as I go into the fight.
My buddies and I will be all right.
We trained and trained to win
this war. No country on earth
will push us anymore.
Though we might be frightened by
enemy unseen, we have on our side
God, who is supreme.
As the shells come screaming and the
bullets come fast, nothing can stop us for
we are in combat at last.
Some men are hit and cry out in pain.
For them, the battle is over, and they are never the same.
As my buddies and I get near
our goal, A shell hits me, and
I'll never grow old. I'll never get
married and have a wife. I'll
never have children, the joy of
my life. There are so many
things I wanted to see,
But fate stepped in; it will never be.
My battle has ended, but my
comrades go on. Nothing can stop
them until the enemy is gone. They
pick up the wounded and bury the
dead. Then a telegram is sent where
it will be read. Tell Dad not to
worry and Mom not to cry.
We'll meet in heaven as the years go by.

Poem written by Frank Naider who lost his brother, Private William Naider (USMC) on June 12, 1945, on Kunishi Ridge, Okinawa.

After almost one full month of some of the bloodiest fighting ever encountered by the United States Marine Corps, Saipan was declared secured by Admiral Turner and General Smith on July 9, 1944. In all, some 3000 Marines and Army infantry lost their lives on the islands. Jack "Jock" Donahoe was one of those brave soldiers. Jock's body was never recovered.

Japanese losses defending the island were in the range of 29,000 to 30,000.

Only two defining forces have ever offered to die for you, Jesus Christ, and the American Soldier. One died for your soul, the other for your freedom. (unknown author)

Note from Author

The story you just read started a few months after my automobile accident in 1991 while recovering from my initial spinal surgeries. It consisted mostly of researching historical events, talking more with my dad, mom, and my Godfather, Jim Murphy, who was only about eight years old when Uncle Jack went off to war. Jim looked up to Jock like he was Bobby Doer, starting 2nd baseman for the Red Sox.

I also read everything I could get ahold of about my family. Once medically cleared, my family life returned to normal with sharing the responsibilities of raising our daughter, Brianne, and son, Sean, with my wife, Diane. Of course, I went back to work for the next twenty-five years and tried to pick up the story where I left off from time to time but found myself going back to the beginning to refresh my memory as to why I wrote this or wrote that. As the saying goes: "Sometimes life gets in the way." I earnestly picked up Uncle Jack's story once again after I retired in 2017 while recovering from additional spinal surgeries. The only difficulty I had was how to write the ending and bring closure for the Donahoes. I just could not find the right words. So, it languished until I received a phone call on April 27th, 2021.

I was on my back patio just sitting on the steps with our labradoodle named Piper when I noticed my phone light up. I did not recognize the number as it displayed an Idaho exchange, so I was just going to ignore it like I do with all calls that I do not recognize. It's an elderly thing, I guess. But something told me to answer it. Warily, I said hello. The gentleman on the other end introduced himself by giving me his full name and occupation, then asked me if I was Robert Donahoe and if I had an uncle that was KIA/MIA on Saipan in 1944. I was visibly shaken for a few seconds but mustered up enough poise to respond and then listen to what he had to say. He was a military researcher, and his job is to try to locate and contact possible relatives of military personnel when remains have been found of those that were killed in action, but their bodies were never recovered. He then continued explaining to me that the effort to recover and identify remains from past wars and conflicts is a joint Department of Defense mission called the Defense POW/MIA Accounting Agency (DPAA). The United States Marine Corps is part of the DPAA. The next thing he said shocked me to the core. Recent remains had been found on Saipan and the government instructed him to reach out to possible relatives that would be willing to participate in DNA testing to identify those remains and bring closure to those families. I had to let all this sink in for a moment but finally said yes. The next step would be for a USMC representative to contact me and to mail out a DNA test kit. They also were able to contact Jack's maternal side of family. As of this writing, we are waiting for the mtDNA results.

Epilogue

My Near Death Experience

(The Reason I wrote this Story)

The sun was unusually brilliant as it peeked over the horizon and reached out its' glaring fingers like a laser beam illuminating the asphalt on the highway. Driving easterly on Route 140 towards New Bedford, Massachusetts, I was about five minutes out from our office located in the Town of Dartmouth, Massachusetts. It was a bitterly cold morning, with just a whisp of cloud cover. My mind was racing with scenarios in anticipation of my meeting with representatives of the local electric utility company (Commonwealth Electric) at our proposed power plant site near the corner of Faunce Corner Road and Old Fall River Road in North Dartmouth.

Traveling at about 65 miles per hour in a 91 Ford Ranger pick-up truck, a cup of Dunkin Donuts coffee straddled between my legs and the radio volume up a little bit higher than normal when suddenly... all control over the steering wheel was gone. It felt like the steering wheel was not connected to the front wheels anymore. The truck started to sway one way, then the other. I struggled to steady the truck but to no avail. It just did not make any sense. The next few seconds seemed to take an eternity. The truck began to swerve sideways, then flipped over onto the driver's side and then up on its' roof and back down onto its' side again. To my bewilderment, I was threading through traffic as the shiny-new, navy blue Ford Ranger pick-up truck slid diagonally across the highway. I was completely disorientated but before I could gather my wits, looming into view was the concrete wall that is supposed to prevent vehicles from landing on the road twenty some 20 odd feet below.

This was it. Not wearing my seatbelt and no airbags, I knew I was probably going die. I had this premonition that the steering wheel was going to go right through me. I cannot quite describe my next feeling, but just before the impact I felt a presence in the cabin with me. Something or someone was holding my right shoulder in place. It felt like someone's hand. It was at that micro-second that the only thing I thought of was my dad's brother Jock.

As the pick-up truck continued its slide on its driver's side, the corner of the front bumper caught a piece of the bridge curbing before continuing its trajectory towards the concrete bridge railing. I braced myself as much as I could for the final impact. The front left corner struck the concrete, and everything in the cabin and in the back of the truck propelled forward. I closed my eyes for what I thought would be my last breath of life. So much is going through your mind at that instant. It is incredible. Your senses are so finely tuned that you swear you feel every heartbeat, hear every background noise, and see every speck of dust on your dashboard but then the noise of the steel and glass crunching into concrete drowns everything out. The truck bounced off the wall and came to a rest with the cab portion exposed to the travel lane. I opened my eyes to see that my briefcase is now an integral part of the shattered windshield. I also noticed there are two other shattered depressions on each side of the windshield. One obviously was where my head struck but the other was unexplainable. I try to move but cannot. The sleeve of my winter jacket has me pinned to the outer frame of the door and the pavement, and the steering wheel is pressed onto my chest. My only view is the bare pavement from where my driver's side window once was. This must have happened when the glass in the driver's door shattered as the truck turned over. My feet are twisted under the brake pedal and accelerator and the back of my head and shoulders are resting against the inside of the caved-in roof. I must have looked like a pretzel. I could feel cold on my left foot, then noticing my shoe was resting between my neck and right shoulder. "How the hell could that happened" I think to myself. I try to move again but the pain in my spine is just too much. I let out a groan. I am completely helpless... and scared.

Something was burning. The acrid smell of whatever it was causes me to panic even more and I cry out. I must have blacked out for a moment because the next thing I hear is a woman's voice.

"Is there anyone still alive?" I yell out.

"Yeah, but I can't get out!"

All I wanted was to get out of this damn truck before it became engulfed in flames. Trapped inside an overturned vehicle with my head mere inches away from the unrelenting traffic whizzing by, I am thinking to myself "What a way to die." I survived a 65 MPH flip-over and crash into a concrete wall only to get decapitated by people who are in a hurry to get to work!

I am cold, thinking that if another vehicle doesn't crash into me then I'll likely just freeze to death. Moments pass when I hear the faint sounds of sirens in the distance. The sirens are getting louder now, and I can breathe in a more normal pattern. The sirens stop but I hear voices and idling vehicles around me. I cannot quite see just exactly what is going on, but I know there is a flurry of activity. A female voice calls out to me, "Sir... sir... can you hear me?"

"Yes" I yell out. "But I'm pinned in."

"Don't move!" the voice replies. "What is your name and are you in any pain?" I give my name and tell her my neck and back hurts. "Okay, this is what we are going to do. I am going to climb through the back window to stabilize you. Try not to move." Within a minute, I feel a woman's hand on my shoulder and her face next to mine. "My name is Melissa," she says, "and my partner's name is Tim. We will get you out of here in no time." I tell her that I smell something burning. "Two of your tires are smoldering," she responds. "There is nothing to worry about."

During those tense moments, the cold and shock start to set in. Melissa covers me with a blanket and continues to ask me questions about my condition. As soon as it became apparent that I have no immediate life-threatening issues, Melissa begins keeping me in conversation, so I don't go into further shock. I tell her I don't know how I lost control of the truck because I was driving in a straight line. "Black ice," she responds. You don't see it 'til it's too late."

Meanwhile she huddles closer to me as best she could under the blanket. You have to envision that the pick-up is on its drivers' side and the passenger side door is facing up towards the sky unable to open because of the force of the crash. So, she had to climb through what used to be the rear window without pushing down on me. I hear her inching her way in. Her upper torso is inside the compressed compartment. Her face is next to mine but in the opposite direction. I could feel her breath, her face, and her hair. I was able to catch a glimpse of her. She had short, dark brown hair with brown eyes. A grin crosses my lips. I am becoming infatuated with her. "Can I call you Robert?" she asks. "Yes... yes, you can."

"Okay, Robert, this is what we are going to do. The fire fighters are going to use a device to cut away the roof. Then they will use another device to remove the roof. It will get a bit noisy, but I will stay with you under this blanket. We need to cover your face in case of any flying glass or metal."

The warmth of her face next to mine returns the grin to my face. The noise of their equipment sounds like a chainsaw, only cutting steel instead of wood. Then the subsequent noise reminds me of an oversized can opener.

The firefighters finish their surgery on the wreck, and somebody yells out, "You now have a convertible." There is some chuckling. As the EMTs prepare to extricate me, Melissa begins to cutaway my jacket and sweater that is keeping me pinned between the pavement and truck.

"I found a donut!" someone calls out. "Can we have it?" I feel embarrassed, thinking to myself "Why couldn't it have been a bagel or something other than a plain, old-fashioned donut?"

Finally, with the roof removed and my jacket and sweater cut away, the EMTs free me from the truck, strap me on a board and fasten a neck brace to keep me immobilized. I see several uniforms scurrying about doing various activities. One of them brings the donut over to me.

"Sorry," Melissa says, "no donuts in the ambulance." That was the last time I saw my donut.

"We are taking you to Saint Luke's Hospital in New Bedford says Tim. "Who can we notify about your accident?" I give them my wife's name and number.

After a battery of tests, x-rays, and the like, I am given a sedative and a painkiller, and then they wheel me into a room for observation.

The hospital room is small with greenish-blue tile on the walls. I look around as best as I can given that I am wearing a neck brace. There is a day calendar on the wall just opposite my bed. It reads January 2nd. The picture on the calendar is that of Saint Christopher.

I start thinking about my uncle Jack again as I struggle to remain conscious from the sedative they gave me. When I wake up, my wife and Dad are in the room with me. They are talking with someone, but I cannot make out who it is or what they were saying. After a few more minutes the person leaves the room and they come over to my bed. Diane is in tears.

I start telling them what happened. Then I look up at my dad and tell him that I was thinking of his brother, Jack, when the accident occurred and that I could feel someone's hand holding me from flying out through the windshield. My dad turned ash gray and just stood there motionless for about a minute. Then he tells me that today is Uncle Jack's birthday. I had no idea.

With no life-threatening injuries, I was released from the hospital the next day with a neck brace and under strict orders to remain in bed until I consult with a neuro or orthopedic surgeon. I felt like I got hit by the proverbial freight train, so I was in no condition to do anything but what the doctor said.

The accident led me to have several surgeries on my spine over the years. Titanium rods, plates, screws, fasteners, and interbody spacers comprise about one third of my spinal column. I am just about unbreakable now. Like I said before, many others have experienced much worse but telling my story helps me to appreciate how fortunate I have been. To this day, some thirty years later, I still do not know how I survived the accident, or for that matter the time in 1972 when I almost drowned getting caught in a flood tide near the former Hugo's Restaurant in Cohasset, Massachusetts. My two best childhood friends' quick action by alerting a man close by in a kayak who reached me and grabbed me by my hair which was under the water, and then pulling me up alongside until Chris and George could pull me onto the shore of the estuary.

All I can say is someone has watched out for me for as long as I can remember. There is absolutely no doubt in my mind that it is my dad's brother, Jack.

ROD AND GUN
By HENRY MOORE

Berry's Hunting Knife on Way To Donahoe in Far off Pacific

Some interesting stories are coming to light under the mounting pile of hunting, fishing and skinning knives being received at the U. S. Marine recruiting headquarters at the Federal building here as a result of this column's appeal a week ago for sportsmen to donate their best blades for the use of Marine Raiders in all part of the world who can't get enough of their favorite in-fighting weapons.

HEATH'S AND BOWEN'S KNIVES OUTWARD BOUND

J. V. Berry of Newcastle, N. H., might be interested to know that the beautiful hunting knife and sheath he sent in this week already are on the way to Pvt. F. C. John W. Donahoe of Brighton, now stationed somewhere in the Pacific.

It seems Donahoe's father Thomas W. Donahoe of 271 North Beacon street, has been searching Boston for weeks following receipt of a letter from his son the main theme of which was "get me a hunting knife somewhere and ship it out here quick." Due to long since frozen stocks Donahoe, Sr., had about given up hope when he saw the Marine appeal.

He didn't have to more than show his son's letter to Sgt. Donald Ross at Marine headquarters before Berry's knife was in his hands and he was on his way down to the Federal building first floor to mail it then and there.

Rod And Gun
By Henry Moore
Berry's Hunting Knife on Way to Donahoe in Far off Pacific

Some interesting stories are coming to light under the mounting pile of hunting, fishing, and skinning knives being received at the U.S. Marine recruiting headquarters at the Federal building here as a result of this column's appeal a week ago for sportsmen to donate their best blades for the use of Marine Raiders in all parts of the world who can't get enough of their favorite in-fighting weapons.

Heath's And Bowne's Knives Outward Bound

J.V. Berry of Newcastle, N.H., might be interested to know that the beautiful hunting knife and sheath he sent in this week already are on the way to Pvt. F.C. John W. Donahoe of Brighton now stationed somewhere in the Pacific.

—

It seems Donahoe's father W. Donahoe of 271 North Beacon Street, has been searching Boston for weeks following receipt of a letter from his son the main theme of which was "get me a hunting knife somewhere and ship it out here quick." Due to long-since frozen stocks, Donahoe, Sr., had about given up hope when he saw the Marine appeal.

—

He didn't have to more than show his son's letter to Sgt. Donald Ross at Marine headquarters before Berry's knife was in his hands and he was on his way down to the Federal building first floor to mail it then and there.

July 11, 1944

BAB 86 GOVT. - WUX Washington D C 11 852 P

WILLIAM J. DONAHOE -

e e 271 North Beacon St. Brighton

Deeply regret to inform you that your son private first
class John W. Donahoe USMCR was killed in action in the
performance of his duty and service of his country no information
available at present regarding disposition of remains temporary
burial in locality where death occurred probable you will be
promptly furnished any additional information received to prevent
possible aid to our enemies do not divulge the name of his ship
or station please accept my heartfelt sympathy letter follows-
A. A. Vandergrift Lieut Genl USMC Commandant US.
MARINE CORPS.

PFC J.W.D. U.S.M.C.
Jack